CLIFFWALK

To my friends
at the Newport
Preservation Society.

Roger Jaeng

Cliffwalk

A Novel of Affairs,
Affluence, and Affection

Roger Farney

Copyright © 2009 by Roger Farney.

Library of Congress Control Number: 2009909124
ISBN: Hardcover   978-1-4415-7250-9
               Softcover   978-1-4415-7249-3

All rights reserved. No part of this book may be reproduced or transmitted in any form or by any means, electronic or mechanical, including photocopying, recording, or by any information storage and retrieval system, without permission in writing from the copyright owner.

This is a work of fiction. Names, characters, places and incidents either are the product of the author's imagination or are used fictitiously, and any resemblance to any actual persons, living or dead, events, or locales is entirely coincidental.

This book was printed in the United States of America.

To order additional copies of this book, contact:
Xlibris Corporation
1-888-795-4274
www.Xlibris.com
Orders@Xlibris.com

58794

Acknowledgments

I would like to especially thank the following people who helped to complete this book.

Katherine Perry-Pyne for featuring her property on the front cover.

Maren Keenan for her ideas, suggestions, and editing.

Hope Marshall of Perception Photography for her work on the cover photo.

Hal Silverman Studio for taking the author portrait.

Cover Models—In Order
Antonina Benvenuto
Ashley Marie DeMar
Jessica M. Rousseau

Chapter 1

June 1928 finds Newport, Rhode Island readying for yet another summer of excess and priceless fun for the well-to-do. Ocean Drive is millionaire's row, where columned mansions line the street like seagulls parade the beach. Each one is built bigger and more extravagant than the one before, showing the owner's mountain of wealth. The summer parties and dances are being planned and finalized; the money for such celebration seems endless.

One of those who is afforded this privilege is Hamilton Morgan Slate III, whose grandfather, Hamilton Morgan Slate I, made a fortune in the shipping and transporting of coal, iron ore, silver, and other cargo across America and the world. With dozens of ships and hundreds of rail cars, he is truly financially blessed. The business legend is now eighty-three years old and each day, more control of the business gradually passes through his tiring hands to his son. Hamilton I is still reluctant to relinquish full control, due to his son's desire to expand the family business. Experience tells him that a ballooning company is self-defeating, hard to manage, and doomed for failure. Hamilton I sees more of himself in his grandson, but because of Hamilton III's youth and his carefree attitude, in addition to his lack of experience, giving him the business would be a financial and family disaster. On the other hand, having Hamilton III more involved (due to his appreciation for the fortune they have) might help preserve the business.

However, at the moment, Hamilton III is a happy-go-lucky, without-a-care, twenty-three-year-old who still favors girls over money. But it always helps when money is never a concern. His mind is alive with activity thinking about last year's summer romance. It was just a five-week affair without the four-letter word. *What could be better*, he thinks. He's much too young for that and besides how could *one* settle for *one*? That would be far too serious.

Hamilton III's Aunt Olive Rose suffered from the childhood affliction Polio and is now confined to a wheelchair. Her mother died young, at only fifty-one years old. Suffering from years of neglect and depression, she basically drank herself to death. After that, Rose's father, Hamilton I, poured himself deeper into his business empire. Rose and her brother, Hamilton II, were left alone much of the time. They were nurtured into adulthood by the household staff who did an admirable job of raising them, but nothing takes the place of a parent's love and guidance. Rose still exhibits much enthusiasm and wit, this perhaps is a mask of her pain and disappointment with what life has dealt her. In different circumstances, she'd probably be married by now and have a family of her own. Rose did have a love affair when she was twenty, but its bitter ending was enough of men for her. It seemed her family money was his first love, not her. Rose holds no ill feelings, and spends most of her days reading about the magic of other people's storybook lives and loves. Rose was beautiful in her youth, but now wears her life through the wrinkles on her face.

Hamilton II is nearly in charge of the home front and the business, and, like his father, work comes first. This led to his wife leaving several years ago, though no one knows for sure the *true story*; she left for a European trip and hasn't been seen since. The rumors can still be heard—"a car accident," "a young French lover," "she jumped off a mountain in Switzerland." A new day, a new story.

The household staff of twenty is busy preparing for another year of pampering this family. Such a large mansion and surrounding property requires a well-organized team of cooks, caretakers, chauffeurs, gardeners, maids, and one dedicated woman in charge to see that nothing is left undone. Hamilton III is sometimes envious of the workers' seemingly simpler life. This can be seen through his conversations with them as he is more like one of their friends than their future boss.

Some of the workers are still at the Connecticut house packing up the remaining essentials. A house for every season is a must for the lifestyle of these privileged Americans. Automobiles and horses now share the roads, streets, and carriage houses. Both are prized possessions. An automobile's honk certainly gives these horses a sense of intimidation and fear, but may never replace a horse's thinking ability to stay on the road. Even President Lincoln could ride one and read at the same time without losing direction.

The staff is busy unloading bags of flour, sugar, ice, and cooking oil at the mansion's hidden side entrance. Men of money cannot tolerate the site of hardworking staff, which results in the building of bunker-entrances and hallways for staff to use. The grandness is left for the family to enjoy without interruption. Ballrooms with gilded chandeliers and marble and wood floors with intricate details showing family names and crests, lions guarding entrances, five-storey columns, second-storey loggias overlooking the ocean—it's all on a grand scale.

Hamilton III sees all of this in a different light than his father and grandfather who simply have to have it all to exist. Hamilton could leave it all behind, or so he thinks; he goes back and forth. His indecision is normally his decision. When Hamilton looks at his father's and grandfather's lack of luster, and sees most of the workers expressing some form of merriment, this adds to his momentary frustration. He soon forgets the emotion when driving his favorite car, a 1925 Bugatti, up and down Ocean Drive, showing off his girl of the moment. With a cigarette in one hand and a pretty girl in the other, affluence has a life of its own.

One long, deep breath through the nose reveals the sweet smells of summer: all of the blooming flowers, the ocean's salty air, and of course, perfume-scented girls. For Hamilton, the latter would be enough to complete any summer, as long as he has one of those girls for romantic fun.

Chapter 2

The kitchen smoke passes the top of the brick chimney on its way to the darkening blue sky. Rose is called to dinner by one of the many bells of this modern mansion. Each year consists of the latest innovative updates. Running water and electricity are the latest. Olive Rose wheels her chair to the top of the third floor stairs where two of the staff help her into the carrying bench and carry her down to the grand entrance.

Hamilton is coming into the entrance at the same time. "Good Evening, Aunt Rose how was your day?"

"It was fine. I started reading a new book entitled *A Summer Love*. It is an absolutely thrilling story of love, lust, and betrayal."

"Is that a book Rose (he calls her by her middle name as do most others) or is that the life of King Henry VIII?"

"I suppose it does resemble the King's life and the shocking events that ensued." She is now in her wheelchair.

"Let *me* push you to the dining room!"

"You should know by now that I won't let you." Wheeling her own chair is one of Olive Rose's last stands of independence. It gives her a sense of needed accomplishment, as she relies on the staff for nearly everything else. There is only one person who she is comfortable allowing to push her chair.

They continue talking as they enter the main dining room with its forty-foot ceiling adorned by four plaster antelopes, a ten-foot crystal chandelier, leather-paneled walls, and a massive hand-cut stone fireplace. Above it hangs Hamilton's deceased grandmother's portrait; his mother's was there when he was younger, but it's now in the attic. Hamilton I and II walk in from the library and join them, with the pungent trail of cigar smoke following them. His grandfather, as of this spring, walks sometimes with the help of a cane. Its top is carved with ivory from an elephant he killed on safari in Northern Africa many years ago. He had a local carver there create the one-of-a-kind piece; ironically it is a lion's head.

"How is my Olive Rose this early summer evening?" asks her father, with his raspy voice.

"I'm in very good spirits," she says.

"Ah, as are we," replies Hamilton I.

But Rose adds, "Your spirits come from a hidden bottle, mine comes from the literary masterpiece I am reading." They share a laugh.

The kitchen staff is busy bringing a wide selection of platters, smoked-fish appetizers, along with duck livers, poached eggs, and freshly baked breads. There is so much food for such a small family. The staff is welcome to divide and take home the leftovers, one of the job's benefits. They no sooner finish with one course and another is delivered. Each dish is palate-pleasing—pork with mushroom gravy, beef with shallots, duck with orange sauce, the freshest vegetables and fruits. Desserts are no less mouthwatering-chocolate pudding, bread pudding, pies, and cakes. All day long the staff cooks and bakes.

Dinner is done and the conversation continues. "How is business, Father?" asks Olive Rose.

"Business is very good, but we need to get your nephew onboard."

Olive continues, "There is a play at the Newport Opera House June fifteenth. Should we attend?"

"Yes," says Hamilton I, "we should. A night-out with the family would indeed be special and I wonder how many more summers I'll have anyway. I'm sure not that many." They have seen a strong, hardened man turn weak in the last few years. "I will inform Mr. Bremhan to buy four tickets first thing in the morning." Mr. Bremhan is Hamilton I's assistant. Hamilton I makes the man work twelve hours a day, but Mr. Bremhan thinks he'll be rewarded someday for it, and works accordingly.

"Let us make our way to the parlor," Hamilton II says. Rose used to only let Hamilton I push her wheelchair, but he is too frail for that now. She really misses it and thus she wheels herself. Hamilton II walks over to a humidor on the side table and takes out two cigars, rolling and cutting the ends. He hands one off to his father. A large flame from a match lights the cigar and the smoke starts to fill the air with its strong odor. Rose hates the smell, but enjoys their company which makes the odor tolerable.

Conversations of work turn to memories of old. "Father, remember when we were in the south of Italy and Hamilton II was chased by that donkey on the farm we were visiting?"

Laughter joins the smoky air. "Yes, I do. It's one of my fondest memories. Mother was alive then and we had a lot of happiness."

He had more happiness, she did not. He found her romantic pleasure as stimulating as making his first million. He eventually turned his attention to making the second million and basically abandoned her needs thereafter. He manages to turn his feelings of guilt to memories of *happier/earlier* days.

Too much of anything is a bad thing and money is just one of them. Hamilton III, after letting the others talk, speaks up.

"Grandfather, I would like to go quail-hunting this summer. My friend Hans Busch is training a new hunting dog, so maybe we could bring them along, too?"

"Yes, that is fine. Do you remember our stockbroker from New York, Harold Cottsman? Well, he mentioned in a recent letter he would be interested in attending one of our hunts. I'll have Mr. Bremhan type a letter off to him. Let's decide on a date. What about for an early birthday, Grandson? It'll be my present to you and on that day I'll give you your own engraved shotgun. Do you prefer Winchester or Remington?"

"You decide, Grandfather."

"Very well!"

"That will be a treasured day, *and* gift," Hamilton adds.

Rose recalls, "I remember Mr. Cottsman. He was here several years ago with his beautiful wife. She looks like a silent film star. Is she not twenty years younger than him?"

Grandfather replies, "Yes, that is true, but unfortunately she was killed by a runaway horse last year while crossing Park Avenue. Very tragic."

"That is an awful story," expresses Hamilton.

Rose yawns and quietly utters, "I am retiring for the evening, everyone. I shall see you in the morning." She rings the bell on the wall and two staff members immediately come to her assistance. They follow her to the grand staircase and lift her into the carrying bench. It's the usual long, hard climb up.

Back into her chair, Rose wheels into the adjoining bathroom to carry out her pre-bedtime ritual. Then back to the bedroom and the waiting staff lift her into bed. She wiggles into her favorite sleep position. Rose soon drifts off to a fairy-tale-come-to-life with her at the center about to marry the most sought-after prince. With excitement she runs through gold-colored fields. She runs and runs . . . but awakes to the reality of having no running legs and no prince. Maybe these dreams help hold her sanity from slipping away.

Chapter 3

The warm morning air is complemented by sweet smells of freshly baked goods that are waiting for them in the breakfast room. Awake is Hamilton who is eager to take the Bugatti out for a spin. He has yet to drive it this year. It is a beautiful Italian automobile simply made for fast driving and he has the goggles to catch the flying mud and bugs. Its horsepower is demonstrated through the sounds and vibrations it produces, much like one of his relationships with a young and adventurous woman.

Many of the rich, and hopefully romance-minded, girls are filling up the neighboring mansions, bringing them to life with ballroom dances, lawn parties, and other social events. This offers the opportunity of flirtations and chance romances for this more-than-willing young man. Hamilton's daydreaming causes him to nearly run off the edge of the cliff; sharply he pulls it back, causing a small dust storm. He continues along past the empty beaches whose waves have no one to splash and where there are no man-made footprints in the sand. Yet.

He stops alongside the ocean, and walks on the beach for a few minutes, remembering last summer's love. Was it just physical romance or love? If he no longer has feelings for her then it must have been romance, not love. Only his body still has feelings for her. Atilda was from Norway; her long, flowing, blond hair would dance like an invitation around her, or at least that's what he read. They had some wild and passionate romance and she still evokes a seduction of the senses. *Will she be here this summer?* He hopes and wonders. The last he heard was that their Newport mansion was up for sale as they had fallen on financial hard times. He picks up a stick, and throws it with all his not-so-great strength into the cold ocean; soon it drops out of sight.

He climbs back into his only real love so far—*the Bugatti*—and heads for home. It's something outsiders call a mansion, but to them it's just a large house they call Seacliff. As he pulls into the long driveway, he sees their Doctor's horse and buggy by the front entrance. He panics momentarily, but remembers Aunt Olive Rose is having her monthly checkup and that she does have some occasional pain medication, which the doctor prescribes.

The doctor is walking out as Hamilton is still sitting in his topless automobile. Hamilton asks, "Is everyone okay?"

"Oh, yes, Hamilton, your Aunt Olive Rose needs her pills."

"Thank God . . . How have you been, Dr. Everhart?"

"Just fine young man, but I have not seen you in several years, and you are overdue for a check up."

"That is true! I will contact you in early fall, before I attend Boston University."

"Very well, Hamilton. I look forward to it. Tell your father and grandfather I said hello."

"Will do, Doctor. Goodbye."

He parks the Bugatti in a stall at the carriage house that was home to a horse just two years earlier. Walking back to the mansion, he can see over in the neighbor's yard. The Oslo P. Smith family has arrived. His two daughters are running around the yard, laughing and having fun. There is an older girl with them, too. *She looks to be seventeen years old or so*, he thinks, *from this distance*. Surely she deserves a closer look. So Hamilton needs an excuse. His quick mind delivers one. He struggles and climbs over the carved limestone wall that's completed with ornate iron work.

"Good day, ladies," he says. With a deliberately lowered gentleman's voice, "Do you need help with anything?"

"Hello, Hamilton."

"Hello, Hamilton III," are the two familiar voices of Oslo's daughters, Herma and Erma.

Herma says, "Help? We have a staff of twenty, would you like to join them?"

"Uh, no. How was your winter, Herma?" Herma, who is the oldest daughter, is now sixteen.

"It was very productive. I'm writing a play called "The Last Dance". Father said it should be well-received."

"Grand. And yours Erma?" Erma is fourteen.

"I learned how to ice skate. I quite enjoy it."

"Very good." He continues talking to the girls, but his eyes are fixed on the new girl. "I am Hamilton Morgan Slate III," introducing himself to her.

"Such a long title. How do you remember it?" answers Emily.

Hamilton melts inside, like an ice cube hitting a glass of whiskey. Her English accent is sophisticated and sweet. "You are . . . ?" he chokingly asks.

"I'm just M."

Erma says, "She's our older cousin from London, England." Mimicking a horn for the Queen's arrival, "Do, do, da, doo . . . now presenting Miss Emily Hope Gloucester. Father thought we should have her over for the summer, as she will be a good influence on us."

"We just call her M," Herma adds.

"How old is older?"

"She is sixteen today, and seventeen next Wednesday." Hamilton likes the seventeen part, but sixteen seems too young. Still Hamilton can't take his eyes off Emily. And she knows it. She keeps her return glances short and almost business-like, thinking a lady never tips her hand.

"It was nice to make your acquaintance, Emily. I hope to see you again soon. Herma and Erma, good day."

The girls giggle and laugh as Hamilton makes his awkward and embarrassing departure. M asks Herma how old Hamilton is.

"I think he's twenty or twenty-one, not sure exactly. Is he not too old for you, M?"

"Perhaps, but he is strikingly handsome." Girlish giggles fill the air. Hamilton exits through their driveway this time. The wall proved to be a little difficult.

Chapter 4

Hamilton is walking on imaginary clouds after seeing Emily. She is the prettiest girl he has ever seen. Her sweet, angelic voice carries like a playing harp. Hamilton is now in a love dream thinking about Emily's mysterious, romantic, and heavenly eyes, and her womanly shape. Someone has been bitten by the *love bug*, or perhaps stung. Time will tell. *Could she be the love of all summer loves?* his youthful mind wonders. He laughs to himself at the irony, that Emily is from England, and his mother studied there many years ago. Perhaps this connection draws him in even closer?

He would love to impress M with his knowledge of London and England, but who could teach him? Hamilton knows Rose reads a lot, so he'll ask for her help. He goes over and rings her room bell. He meets Rose by her bedroom and follows her to the room's balcony that overlooks the ocean.

"What's on your mind?"

"Well, uh . . . I would like to learn about London and England."

"Why the interest? Are you traveling abroad this year?"

"No."

"Then why?"

"One of our neighbors next door, Oslo, has a relative staying there, and they are from London. I thought it would help me get to know them better if I know something about the area and the country."

Rose smiles. "A relative? Well *they* must be a girl, Hamilton, or you would have no interest . . . Tell me I'm right. Is she a doll?"

"You are right, Aunt Rose, but I would like to be her friend."

"You don't have any girls for friends, but you do have a few girlfriends . . . Hamilton you're a sly young man. If she's too young, you will get yourself in trouble. Remember that Vanderne boy Ernold, who is now living in Milan, Italy? He impregnated that fifteen-year-old girl. The poor fool wanted to marry her until his father sent him to Italy for five years as punishment."

"I remember that. I will not do anything careless or stupid like that."

"Okay, then . . . London . . . Go down into the library and get that book *Famous European Cities*. It's on the left side halfway down. Bring it to me."

Hamilton walks down and brings the large book back. Rose starts the learning lesson. "Let's familiarize you with some famous landmarks and then we'll move to kings and queens."

Three hours of listening to Rose giving him the highlights: his mind is full, and she senses it. "That's enough for today. Would you like to continue tomorrow?"

"I would like that. I do appreciate your help, Aunt Rose." What he doesn't know is that she enjoys giving the information more than he appreciates receiving it.

Dinner hour finds the family eating together—a rare occurrence. Rose teases Hamilton about the girl next door.

"Father . . ."

"Yes?"

"Young Hamilton has an interest in learning about London, England."

"I'm glad something piques his interest."

"Oh! It's not some*thing*, it's some*one*."

"Son, you need to leave the girls alone and concentrate on your upcoming studies at Boston University. I will pay dearly for your privilege to attend there!"

"Yes, sir, I'll be ready," but he thinks of nothing else but the girl whose eyes could melt the snowcaps on Mount Everest. He continues eating and flashes a thanks-a-lot to Olive Rose, who returns a half smile.

"Grandfather, let's play billiards after we are done eating. I sure do miss the days when your old friends played here," Rose says. Rose plays too, but they prop her up to shoot.

Hamilton's mind comes back to Emily, *I will have to go over there tomorrow and see her*. She is more arousing than those risqué dancers he and his friends closely watched two years ago when they were in Paris. Still daydreaming, his temperature now skyrockets and he turns red in the face.

Grandfather raises his voice, "Young Hamilton . . . Young Hamilton, are you going to join us for billiards?"

"Yes . . . Yes . . . I was just thinking."

He follows them to the Great Room, with its massive stone fireplace and intricate tiled floor. There is a large custom chandelier adorned with a hunting scene of a fox being chased by hounds. The billiard table is priceless—Hamilton I had it commissioned by an Italian carver. The wood is olive burl, one of the rarest in the world; other rare species are intertwined as well. It is finished off with gold accents and cost more than five of their workers' yearly pay twenty years ago. Now it's worth a great deal more.

Grandfather says, "I shall play against young Hamilton and Rose, then the winner will play Hamilton II." He racks up the balls, like a well-seasoned gambler, pushing them around until they're just perfect.

"Young Hamilton, you can break." He does, not one goes in. Grandfather goes to work. Although he's frail, he's a tough opponent. In goes the number three ball, then the number five ball, and then three more in quick succession before he misses a shot. Hamilton helps Rose and she sinks two. Grandfather misses a tough bank shot—Rose sinks three more to even the count. Hamilton sinks another, so does Grandfather. Rose makes a run and is shooting the number eight ball on a difficult shot; she sends it down the pocket for victory. Perhaps Grandfather was playing too easy.

With two more drinks and more smoked cigars, it's bedtime for the Hamilton men. "Good night . . . Good night. Rest well . . . Sleep tight," adds Grandfather with some nostalgia, referring to the fact that some early beds indeed had ropes on them that needed to be tightened.

Chapter 5

Morning light, warm breezes, and thoughts of Emily awaken young Hamilton. He can't wait to go next door, but it's only six a.m. He heads down to the breakfast room. An array of smells—coffee, eggs, meat, and fruit—welcome him.

"Good *early* morning," one of the staff says. They're not accustomed to seeing him at this hour; two hours later is the norm. Rose makes her way into the room and nearly falls out of her chair seeing Hamilton up already.

"Somewhere to go?" she asks.

He smiles and joyfully declares, "Life is grand and it just keeps getting better." They laugh.

The staff is busy in the kitchen—cooking sausages and bacon and eggs, cutting up beef for dinner, plucking chickens, and dicing pork for a Mediterranean stew. The pastries are stacking up, along with other delectable desserts, some topped with exotic fruits. The work is hard and the days are long, but these lucky people are paid more than other workers outside the mansion. If someone proves to be a good employee, Hamilton I rewards them, but an incompetent worker is fired immediately. This knowledge keeps them on their toes, and on their best behavior.

Rose and Hamilton have a good talk in between bites of breakfast. Rose writes some poetry and a few pieces have been published. "Are you working on any poetry, Rose, or are you just reading these days?"

"I have started writing some new poetry, but I can't seem to finish anything..." Rose gets easily frustrated and loses interest in her work, then she can only concentrate long enough to read someone else's work.

Rose asks, "What time would you like to continue your study of London and the English culture?"

"It would have to be early afternoon. I have unfinished business this morning..."

"I'm sure you do... You should buy a *Harpers Bazaar* magazine for that young woman. They feature great stories and the latest fashions. She would enjoy it, I'm sure."

"A superb suggestion, Aunt Rose. I shall make my way downtown and buy one. I will see you right after lunch, say one thirty?"

"Yes, okay. Good day."

He exits through the rear of the house, skip-walking across the lawn with excitement, opens the carriage house door, and starts his fine automobile. It's idling in the driveway and he sees Cleveland Roosevelt Jr., a sixteen-year-old black boy. His father is their chauffeur and has worked for Hamilton's grandfather for over twenty years. These days, he drives them around in the Duisenberg. Before that, and now just on special occasions, he chauffeurs them with the horse and carriage, which is a sight to see. The younger Roosevelt is following in his father's footsteps and is in-training. His father is still in good health, but he is sixty-two years old and wants to retire to a life of fishing and relaxing.

Cleveland is polite and very well-spoken; his father has taught him well and encourages him to read a lot. Cleveland and his father are polishing the Duisenberg.

"Good morning, Mr. Roosevelt. How are you?"

"Fine, Hamilton..." Sr. responds.

"It's a beautiful summer day," Jr. says and adds, "Taking the Bugatti out for a drive? It's a work of art, sir!"

"Yes, it is," Hamilton agrees. He is not pretentious like some other wealthy people. He can see Cleveland's liking of life's finer things.

"Would you like to go, Cleveland? I'm just going downtown for a magazine. We will be back in less than thirty minutes."

Cleveland asks his father. "If Hamilton says it's fine, then you go."

Cleveland smiles and climbs in. "You'll need these." Hamilton hands him a pair of goggles. He shows off and spins up a little of the green lawn, laughing as he does it.

Out onto Ocean Drive, he accelerates quickly and looks over at Cleveland, who is enjoying this slice of feeling like a rich man. He parks the automobile downtown across from the harbor and its mooring sailboats. Hamilton's family also has a sailboat, but it's seldom used because they have so many other things to do.

He runs into the store and comes back out sporting the *Harpers Bazaar* magazine. He's happier than a man in a hardware store. Cleveland looks over and gives him a puzzled look. After all it's perceived to be a woman's magazine. Hamilton notices his look and quickly says, "Oh! It's for a friend of mine."

"Okay," says Cleveland, as he laughs softly. Soon they're back at the carriage house.

"Thank you, Hamilton, for the ride."

"Anytime!" Hamilton calls as he walks away.

He enters the house through the back. Going over to the kitchen area, he asks one of the staff to wrap it as a gift. She does and it's finished with a hand-tied bow. Hamilton walks back out to the side yard and peers over at Oslo's yard. The girls are not outdoors yet. He completes this nervous exercise of going back and forth until he sees Herma and yells over.

"Herma, is Emily around?"

Herma is wise beyond her years, "Why do you ask?"

"Oh . . ." he says, with a reddened face, "I have a magazine for her."

"I will request her presence for you. I'll be right back." The three girls are now visible walking across the lawn towards him. Emily then approaches by herself.

"You wanted to see me?"

"Uh-uh! Yes."

"Why?" she says with an unrevealing partial smile.

"I have a magazine for you."

"Did I ask you for one?" she says in a standoffish tone.

"No, but I thought it would give you some insight on American culture and fashion, that's all." She senses his interest is in more than her knowledge of American fashion.

"Are you wanting something else?"

"I, uh . . . I, uh . . . Like you."

"Are you flirting with me young Hamilton?"

"I guess I am."

"I've seen boys like you before. They only want a good time, and then they move on to the next pony in the stable." Hamilton realizes she's not naïve, but there's something about her that's drawing him in. Emily finds him to be handsome, but she doesn't trust his motives.

Hamilton is holding the wrapped magazine behind his back and pulls it out. "It is Christmas," she says laughing. He hands it to her.

"Thank you. I will read it later, but I must return to the mansion. We are getting ready for a jazz ball here next week. It is a celebration for my seventeenth birthday. Did you get an invitation?"

"I'm not positive, but I'll check with the staff."

"If not, I guess you are welcome to attend, and on that day you can come back with *another* wrapped gift. Goodbye, Hamilton." She is short and to-the-point, but her sweet, soft voice plays over and over in his head as he walks back home.

He is very pleased with the outcome of this awkward, and planned, encounter. She is more of an attraction now than even yesterday's first meeting. She spoke the word *flirt*. He keeps thinking about that, and all of the words she said. He goes to the kitchen area where the staff is busy with daily chores. Mrs. Beverly Jones is in command of this household operation. She collects and sorts the mail, directs the staff, prepares menus, along with a host of other daily activities and duties.

"Mrs. Jones, did we receive an invitation from the Oslo P. Smith family concerning a jazz ball?"

"Yes we did, and I gave it to your father. But since when have you been interested in dances and balls?"

Rose interrupts, "Since the new girl arrived next door."

"It's true I have a liking for her, but I need to become more refined, and attending social gatherings is a step in that direction."

"I shall ask your father for the invitation and pencil it in on your schedule."

"Thank you, Mrs. Jones."

Chapter 6

Lunch is being served. The menu changes daily, another of Mrs. Jones's tasks. Lunch is a near-limitless variety of meats, salads, vegetables, freshly baked muffins, breads, soups, crackers, drinks, and desserts. With lunch over, Rose and Hamilton are diving into the complex study of kings and queens, the monarchy, prime ministers, the days' fashions, the foods, the drinks, and the country's struggles and triumphs. The afternoon evaporates quickly. Rose and Hamilton are truly enjoying this study and their newfound closeness.

Rose says with a sardonic flair, "Have your studies made an impression on the young lady yet, or is it London Bridge is falling down, falling down?" she starts singing.

"I think she's impressed. She seems to like me and our conversation."

"Has it led to, at least, a mouthwatering, sweet kiss?" Hamilton laughs and retorts, "One should never kiss and tell, and I think it's almost time to eat." They both laugh as he exits the room.

Evening swiftly announces its presence as dinner is now being served, with only Rose, Hamilton, and Grandfather present. Hamilton II is away in Boston on business. Their growing empire takes a lot of hard work. Young Hamilton announces he is tired and going up to his room to read.

Once there, he takes out a magazine, and is just looking at all of the photos showing pretty girls, which starts him thinking about Emily. She consumes his thoughts. It is now eight thirty and he cannot sleep. He decides to take a stroll along Cliffwalk, as it is a beautiful summer evening.

Along the walk he comes face-to-face with a young woman he met two years earlier. She's now twenty years old. Her family owns a summer cottage, not a mansion. It's quaint and unassuming compared to the granite masterpieces around it.

"Is that you, Hamilton?"

"Wow! Hello, Dedra. Dee Dee, it has been two summers, hasn't it?"

"Yes."

"Are you in school?"

"I am attending a small college in Boston. It's a glorified finishing school." She makes it seem less important.

"And you, Hamilton?"

"I'm finally going to Boston University this fall. I am out for a restless night's walk as I can't seem to sleep. Oh well, it's still early."

"Could I join you?"

"Yes, I would be honored."

The walk along the ocean is slow and the conversation is fast. Dedra says, "I did miss not seeing you last summer. My grandmother was ill, and has since died. I spent as much time with her as I could."

"I'm sorry to hear that."

"Thank you." She now has a couple of tears running down her cheek. Hamilton, without thinking, starts to move them away with his fingers.

"You are a gentleman." She reaches out and takes his hand. She then leans in, and gives him a most welcoming kiss on the side of his mouth. He responds and kisses her on the lips, as his hand slides around her curvy waist.

"Oh! You feel heavenly, Hamilton. It has been so long since I have touched a man, I'm sorry, but I may not be able to stop." The kisses and touching prove to be too uncontrollable and too passionate. With the moonlit sky, the smell of summer flowers, and the crashing waves of the ocean, Hamilton gives in to his and her desires. Pleasures of the mind and body are felt as love's lightning strikes.

The woman he just seduced is lying on the ground next to him. Her naked self is being illuminated by the early evening moon, revealing her petite body and breasts. He can still taste her perfumed skin on his lips. *I feel so good, but I feel so bad*, he thinks. How could he do this to Emily? He got so caught up in the moment that he forgot about the larger picture. The quick emotion called lust leads him into longer feelings of guilt.

"Oh, Hamilton, it has been a long time since I have felt a man naked. I feel so good. You are very pleasing." Dedra is lying there in complete satisfaction, not wanting to move.

"Should we head back, Dedra?" trying to hurry her. They hear voices coming closer as they lie on the grass of a neighbor's mansion. A couple of dogs bark.

Quickly they dress, jump up, and do a fast short walk. She kisses him on the lips and says, "I hope to see you again soon. This was complete fun. You do remember where I live, don't you?"

"Yes, I do. Good night, Dee Dee." A quick hug. They separate, and begin their walks back. Hamilton is guilt-ridden; he thinks about Emily and his impulsiveness with Dedra. How could he be so despicable? Surely he will be chastised for it.

He enters through the side entrance, walks past the kitchen and into the main hall where he runs into his grandfather.

"Hamilton, I thought you went to bed hours ago?"

"Well, I couldn't sleep and went for a walk."

"Did you fall down? You have mud on your pants."

"I did slip." *Indeed I did*, thinking to himself.

"Would you join me for a night cap?"

"Sure, Grandfather" He needs a drink or two or three, so he can try to forget about this night.

"What is your choice, young man? Oh, here's a bottle of scotch from 1905. This damn stuff costs as much as my first horse. Hey, let's toast to that horse. He lived to be twenty-three years old. Bottoms up!"

His Grandfather is a seasoned drinker. He is not. With two down the pipes and the third one nearly finished, Hamilton feels the effects, but it's helping him forget the night's earlier episode.

He pours the fourth one and it goes down slow. Grandfather is ready for the fifth. Even at eighty-three and frail, he is still tough. They both slide back into their chairs, enough to say, that's all I can drink. Grandfather falls asleep in the chair. Hamilton attempts to wake him, but it's no use. Hamilton weebles and wobbles, slowly making his way through the grand hall and up the flights of stairs. Resembling a broken-winged bird, he comes close to falling several times.

The morning comes with a hangover headache. It's a rainy day and it pours, as does Hamilton's guilt. He finally goes down to the kitchen. It's nearly eleven.

"Would you like breakfast or lunch, Hamilton?" asks Mrs. Jones.

"Neither, I would like an aspirin and a soda water."

"You should eat something or you may vomit. But then, your grandfather had the same breakfast as you, and he went back to be up at nine o'clock. Was it a long night?"

"It was." Taking her advice, he has a bite of toast and heads back to bed. Lying there, he thinks about Emily, trying not to feel guilty. But then why should he feel that way? He is not in a relationship with her, or does a mental one count? What if she finds out? Then he'll never get close to her. For her, his heart beats faster with each thought. For last night's rendezvous, it only beat fast for a few minutes. Could Emily be the first girl he's ever been in love with? Or is she the first girl he's wanted to be in love with? His mind is working overtime on limited sleep.

He spends the day in bed, napping, thinking, and reading. A magazine filled with items for sale gives him the idea to give Emily an unforgettable birthday present. He'll bring it to the jazz ball. She'll be impressed, but what shall he buy? A tiara or perhaps a crystal vase, perchance two tickets to a play? What would say "I care and look at me." Maybe Rose would know, or Mrs. Jones. She has great ideas. He thinks and thinks, *I will buy her a . . . pearl necklace. Yes she can wear it at the ball.* He will give her the gift the morning of her birthday. He must find out what she's wearing for a gown. *Maybe she'll be in a flapper dress.* The pearls will compliment that look. Even the rich have their worries.

It's six p.m. and Hamilton has no physical motivation, just mental alertness, as he is obsessed with the new girl next door. The catalog is full of interesting things for sale, just not pearls. Tomorrow, he will go downtown to the jeweler, they should have it. He's too tired even for dinner.

Rose knocks on his bedroom door, "Hamilton, are you okay?"

"Yes, I am just a little sick today."

"Hmm . . . So is Father. I'll see you in the morning then."

"Okay, good night, Rose."

Chapter 7

Today finds Hamilton glad to be alive and feeling like a new man. He's up at five a.m. A quick bath, and a straight-razor shave which produces just a little nick and only two drops of blood. He dresses into his laid-out clothes left there by the household staff. Some days he still chooses his own. The stores don't open their doors until eight a.m., so he has nearly two hours to fill. He needs a full breakfast after not eating much yesterday. Three eggs for protein is what he has the kitchen deliver, with two pieces of toast, and a tall glass of freshly squeezed orange juice, all welcomed by his empty stomach. Mrs. Jones comes in daily at seven a.m., and she doesn't leave until six p.m. She has more than enough to do to fill that time, and more. Some days she takes work home or just stays later. She works for the family all year as does most of the other staff, except for the extra gardeners and maintenance people.

Hamilton looks at the time on his gold pocket-watch. The stores open in fifteen minutes, so it's time to leave. The sun is up high already, producing a warm summer morning. On the drive, he thinks about Emily. He would love to seduce her, but he also wants a relationship. So he is willing to forego a one-time tryst. He wonders if her kiss will be as sweet as her lips look and if her skin will be soft and smell of flowered French perfume when he kisses it? And . . . he needs to watch the road and the pedestrians crossing it.

He pulls into a parking spot, exits the automobile, and enters the jeweler's shop. He's been here before; he purchased a necklace for his mother one year for Christmas. The jeweler does not recognize him.

"Good morning, sir. Let me know if I can help you."

"You can. I'm looking for a pearl necklace, as a birthday gift."

"How old would the lady be?"

"She is turning seventeen."

"Then you would want a string of petite pearls. Older ladies like the larger ones."

"That makes sense," agrees Hamilton.

"Do you want it to be just pearls, or do you want something Art Deco, say a pearl then a piece of gold then a pearl?"

"Not sure. No . . . I think I'll stay with just pearls."

"Well, here's a one-of-a-kind, rare piece with whole and multicolored pearls, although it's a lot more expensive," the jeweler glances out the front window at his expensive Buggati.

"Yes, that one is fine. Could you gift-wrap it?"

"Yes, I sure can." He gives the jeweler most of the money he has, leaving him with only a couple of dollars. *That's fine*, he thinks, *I am trying to impress her.*

He drives around the town for a little while. A couple of girls wave to him and a group of older boys yell *race car*. It's an impressive automobile. He pulls into the long entrance at home. The men are clipping the hedges, and redoing and mortaring some of the stone work. They are busy making his existence easier. *He's lucky to have this life of luxury*, he thinks. Hamilton walks in the front door past the guarding granite lions and the large floor vase with its freshly cut flowers.

Mrs. Jones is walking towards him and hands off a note. "The young lady next door brought it over early this morning just after you left."

Inside is an invitation just for him written in type, with his name on it:

> Dear Hamilton,
> You are very thoughtful and I wanted to say thank you for the magazine. I hope to see you at the ball.

His heart races with excitement, as does the rest of his body; he's aroused and red in the face. Mrs. Jones says, "I would give anything to be young and wealthy like you, Hamilton. Enjoy it while you can. Adulthood and responsibility will soon be upon you."

Hamilton is shining like a pair of well-polished shoes. Rose is being carried down the stairs and notices Hamilton's beaming smile.

"Looks like someone found a lost puppy or did someone find love?"

"I'm just a happy young man, Rose,"

"Are you sure Emily's not a *femme fatale*?"

Hamilton laughs and replies, "No, unfortunately she is the opposite of seductive and she does not appear to be dangerous."

"Time will tell," she cautions and heads to the kitchen for lunch.

Hamilton takes the gift up to his room and places it inside a dresser. He is too excited and anticipatory to have an appetite for lunch. He heads back downstairs and goes into the library, finding a fiction novel named *Affluence, Affairs, and Affection*. Rose mentioned the book had some good love passages in it, and maybe he could find some helpful sentences to use in impressing the new girl. He skips around and reads some of the pages.

Her skin tasted like honey straight from the comb itself, so fresh and pure.

Is this fair, he wonders, to use words from a book and not the instant thoughts in your mind? Or maybe thoughts are not instant or innocent. They are trained and developed by what you've read or experienced your whole life? He reads on.

His hands followed her neck, making their way down past the shoulders, softly touching the outside of her breasts, just enough to play with her senses in a teasing way . . . She then melts with excitement as his hands continue, finally reaching her point of no return.

He can't read any more of the book; it's making him think of the other night with Dedra, and not Emily. It fills his head with these pleasured thoughts, which turn to feelings of guilt. To ease his thoughts, he gets the idea to clean and wax the Bugatti. So he crosses the green lawn to the carriage house, where Cleveland and Cleveland's father are gathered.

"Good afternoon, Mr. Slate," says the senior Roosevelt.

"Please call me Hamilton." He's not pretentious and realizes his luck in life.

"Hello, Hamilton," says Cleveland Jr.

"Hello men, are you driving Grandfather today in the Duisenberg, or by horse and carriage?"

"Pretty much the Duisenberg these days," responds Sr., adding, "It's mighty fancy, mighty fancy."

"Do you have polish out here? I want to make my automobile look new again."

"Sure do," Sr. says. "Cleveland is done and he can help you."

"Thank you."

Sr. walks in and finds the polish, handing it to Cleveland Jr., along with a pail.

Jr. offers his help, "I'll get the water." He goes to the hand pump and fills it up, then places the pail next to the Bugatti. Cleveland and Hamilton toss the sudsy water around the automobile with their sponges, while asking each other questions.

"Are you in college yet, Hamilton?"

"This fall."

"How is high school?"

"It's good. He [Father] is proud of my grades. I'm in the top ten percent of my class. Are you going to college?" Hamilton asks, without thinking it's probably too expensive for him.

"No, I will have to work. I want to work for your family. That will be a good life." Hamilton thinks to himself, *it's unfortunate that a young man that smart can't go to college.* Maybe he should talk to Grandfather about it. They continue drying off the Bugatti, talking more, then applying the polish. "Sure be shiny," says Cleveland, downplaying his knowledge of language.

Hamilton overheard Cleveland and his father talking one day without them knowing his presence. He's as smart as most of these rich children, but he doesn't want to be seen as a cock-a-doodle-do-er.

The polish is so shiny that Hamilton can see a reflection of a girl in its mirror-like finish. He turns around with inquisitive excitement thinking it maybe Emily. *Oh no,* he thinks to himself, *it's Dedra.* She is wearing a thin summer dress that's far above her calves, looking at him with her wide and inviting seductive smile.

"Hamilton did you forget where I live?"

"No, no. I'm just busy with these summer activities." Cleveland excuses himself and goes over to where his father is changing the oil in the Duisenberg.

"Can you see me tonight?" she asks. "Or should I come over later? I'll knock on your front door, say, around eight?"

Hamilton doesn't want to take the chance that Emily or Rose would see Dedra there so he reluctantly agrees to meet her later. "Um, I can meet you at nine," thinking Rose will be asleep and not hear or see him leave the house. Hopefully the same holds true with Emily next door. Hamilton thinks, *What am I doing? The last time I followed an impulse, I felt, and still do, feel guilty. What am I doing?* And then thinking this is the best course of action to get rid of her, "I will meet you by Ocean Bluff, next to Granite House. See you then." He hurries her away.

Chapter 8

Hamilton will meet her, but nothing can happen. He will control himself, he'll behave, and he won't have anything to feel guilty about. Again. Can he do it? Now, young Hamilton has doubts—she looks so tempting, so willful. So no one will know. If he just gives in this one time, then he will tell her he can't see her again, because he likes someone else. That will work. The more he thinks the more he's confused. It's a long afternoon. He occasionally goes into and looks out the guest bedroom's side window to see if Emily is home, but there is no afternoon activity next door. Maybe they left for the day?

Rose knocks on his door, "Did you want to continue the lessons of London?"

"No thank you, I am really tired, I awoke this morning at five. I am going to take a short nap."

"Well, let me know if you change your mind."

"Thank you! I will." He lies down, but his mind can't locate sleep.

He gets up and it is dinner time. His father is back in town, so he must make the effort to join them. He joins them and everyone is already there eating dinner.

"He's alive!" his father jokes.

"I got up too early and I'm not accustomed to that."

"Up early!" Grandfather rasps. "Early is up at four-thirty, seven days a week and then twelve-hour days at the office, working until your eyes get blurry. You will soon find out."

"How was the trip to Boston, Father?" inquires Hamilton trying to divert his Grandfather's sarcasm away from him.

"Very productive. We are acquiring a small company that repairs our locomotives. It'll save us a half-million dollars over the next ten years." It may, but Grandfather doesn't like the incurred debt that goes along with it.

"Did they negotiate any more?" Hamilton I asks.

"No, we had to up our price a little because they had another bidder." Grandfather doesn't like that answer so it's best to stop asking any more business questions. Rose requests, "It's a beautiful summer evening. Can we go out to the tea house?"

The tea house is seldom used. It is a Japanese-inspired architectural treasure with a serpent-shaped roofline, which is red and green with gold accents, with each side of the roof curved like wings. The windows have unique shapes and the inside is unusually charming. It was full of life when Hamilton's mother was still alive. She would entertain her friends for hours. She let life consume her while most other people consume life.

They are now in the tea house. Hamilton looks at his pocket-watch. Rose wonders, "Somewhere to go?"

"No, I am really tired," he fibs.

His father adds, "The poor boy was up at five a.m. We should call the doctor. Ha-ha!" He pulls out a cigar and lights it up. The first puff gives a pleasant smell, the next an odor, then the rest resemble the stink of a skunk. He goes over by the doorway and rings the bell for the house staff who come quickly.

"Good evening, Mr. Hamilton. What would you like, sir?" The woman looks back and forth at all three of the Hamilton men while she's speaking.

"I'll have a scotch whiskey on the rocks. Make it a double. I wish to sleep like a baby," Hamilton I requests.

Hamilton II agrees, "I'll have the same, but make mine a single."

Hamilton is tired and thinks of the nine p.m. rendezvous, "I would like tea. We are in the tea house!" he chirps with a cheap joke. Rose asks for a glass of milk and a pile of those chocolate-covered wafers. They talk, eat, and drink for an hour.

Hamilton is getting a little nervous as it's after eight o'clock and everyone is still out here, not mentioning yet that they are getting tired. He should go first and maybe they will follow.

"Well, it is getting late. I'm falling asleep just sitting here. Good night all!" he says.

Rose then asks Hamilton, "Could you help me back to the house. It is a little dark out." Hamilton walks next to her. She wheels up the back ramp into the house and down the hall. Hamilton finds two of the staff and they lift her up the flights of stairs. Hamilton follows and goes into his room.

He can see the lights are still shining in the tea house. Now he figures he must sneak out the side entrance. Hopefully the staff won't see him. It is eight forty-five, and he doesn't need Dedra showing up at the front door. He softly makes his way out of the bedroom, into the hall, and down the stairs.

He hears voices as he reaches the bottom stair. *Oh no! It is Father and Grandfather.* He slides and tucks himself into the opening at the bottom of the large staircase. He holds his breath and does not move. They walk on by and go up the stairs. He looks down the hall by the side entrance. No sight of the staff, so he makes his way out slowly.

Hamilton proceeds down the side yard walking along, and almost in, the hedge, hoping that his hedge-walk and the near-darkness make him obscure. Walking along Cliffwalk, he continues making his way to Ocean Bluff where Dedra will be waiting. He keeps thinking, *This is irresponsible, I have no feelings of love for this girl, just lust.* Hamilton is caught between a rock and a hard place, but is still proceeding like a fox to a chicken coop.

He is almost there and sees Dedra walking towards him. "Oh Hamilton, I knew you would come," she says in a sweet girlish voice. "Do you like me?" she asks.

"Yes I do, Dee Dee or I wouldn't be here," now lying to two people.

"Oh, you are a Prince. Where is your white horse? I am your Lady, my majesty." She continues romantically role-playing. "Kiss me, my long-lost love." She moves in closer, as does Hamilton. He kisses her in a dominating way and she responds with her own vigor.

He gently eases her onto the grassy ground, rubbing her leg with his eager hand. She whispers into his ear, "Love me like I'm the last woman on earth and the world is coming to an end." She lifts up her dress revealing her nakedness. The hot summer night just got a little hotter. He plunges into her wanting body. The feelings are beyond words, but not beyond their sounds of satisfaction.

"Oh, Hamilton you are a great lover," she says as they lie there.

"You feel heavenly, Dee Dee."

"Will I see you tomorrow night, Hamilton?"

"Uh, uh, uh . . . I have to study. It's been four years since I attended school, so I need to devote more time to that."

"Are you sure you don't have another lover?" she jokingly asks.

"No! No! But I need to go home and sleep. It has been a long day," avoiding the question.

"Well, okay. I want to see you again, you know," she says, obviously looking for more of Hamilton's time and attention.

"I'm sure it won't be too long."

"You please me," she says softly. He kisses her on the side of her mouth.

"Don't be a stranger, my love. Goodnight," she sweetly whispers in his ear. Dedra turns and heads for home. Hamilton walks the short distance home accompanied by his two familiar friends—satisfaction and guilt—both vying for control of his thoughts; while his body only knows the pleasure he had, and still feels it. He falls into his bed, finding sleep as fast as a shooting star.

Chapter 9

Hamilton wakes to a chirping bird's visit to his balcony. It is a pleasant sound and he is well-rested from a satisfying night of sleep—and other satisfactions. He gets out of bed, stretches and yawns at the same time. He smells Dedra's perfume still on his skin, so he takes a quick bath.

Breakfast will taste great, he thinks, so off to the kitchen he journeys. Grandfather is having a bad day and even with the cane it's hard to navigate the stairs. Rose is at the bottom of them in her wheelchair.

"Father, may be you need to borrow my wheelchair," she says trying to give him the subtle hint that he also needs one. But she knows her father is very stubborn and would crawl first.

"I don't need one, Rose. I am as strong as I have ever been." But his words are not convincing, not even to himself.

Hamilton walks down the hallway by the kitchen. He can see out the side window into the yard next door. Dozens of workers are gathered there, putting up a large canvas tent, some of its wooden poles still lay on the ground and appear to be twenty feet long. *They must be getting ready for the ball, which takes place in two days*, he thinks.

He continues and walks into the breakfast room with its irresistible smells coming from the adjacent kitchen.

"Good morning, sir." He is welcomed by an attentive staff member.

"Good morning, Mr. Avery," who's a cook. "What'll it be this fine day?"

"I'll have my usual dose of eggs, bacon, toast, coffee, and orange juice."

"Yes, sir, I'll fry them right up."

The cook enters the kitchen. With one hand he breaks open the eggs and they slide into a pool of butter. He quickly starts the bacon in another pan. He's a master of his craft.

Rose and Grandfather are now in the breakfast room talking with Hamilton.

"Good morning." Grandfather's voice sounds of his frustration and failing health.

"Good morning, Grandfather," says Hamilton, adding some extra enthusiasm to try and cheer him up, if that is possible. "I see they're setting up next door for the jazz ball," Hamilton adds.

Grandfather replies, "That will be a grand time. I remember our many and unique dances. God damn, those were the good old days." You can see a tear in his eyes.

"I remember a few of those," Rose says.

"Which was your favorite, Grandfather?" Hamilton asks.

"Ah! It was the Venetian ball, the colorful and festive costumes and all the unique masks. Why, it was the largest of all the mansion dances at that time. Drinking liquor was legal then. People from New York, Boston, Chicago, and all of the wealthy folks from here in Newport attended. We celebrated and danced, ate and drank until sunrise. I still have boxes of the thank-you notes we received stored in the attic. Time goes by so fast, it seems like yesterday."

Hamilton encourages, "Well you can't take away those memories."

"You are right," Grandfather says, and adds, "In the end all you can take are those memories, not the money, the mansions, the jewels. Just the memories."

Hamilton cuts in, "Well, Grandfather and Aunt Rose, I'm going to check out the activity next door."

Rose wisely wonders, "The activity next door? Or the *girl* next door?" They all smile.

"Good day," Hamilton quickly walks down the side hall and out onto the open side porch.

The workers next door have the tent half-up and the wooden poles extend beyond the height of the tent, leaving room for festive-colored flags. One is in place, showing a rampant lion in gold with a green-and-red background. Massive flower pots are being placed in strategic locations. This will indeed be the most talked-about summer event, leaving a lasting impression for all of those lucky enough to have an invitation.

Chapter 10

Hamilton continues to gaze next door and his mind daydreams. He smiles and kisses Emily's hand. *My lady, may I have this dance with a woman so lovely as you?* They dance on clouds over the mansion.

"Hamilton, Hamilton." Rose yells out the door and wakes him up. "Are you sleeping?"

"No, no, just deep in thought."

"Okay. Did you want to learn more about England today?"

"Yes! I'll meet you in the library at two p.m?"

"Okay. See you then." Rose wheels away.

Hamilton continues to dream of kissing Emily, her natural pink lips, so luscious, so inviting. He hears a voice, "Hey Hamilton. Hamilton."

It is Cleveland, scaring him out of another of his daydreams. "Father and I had to get some oil from your stall of the carriage house and we see a girl, she's sleeping in your Bugatti. Should we call the authority?"

"No, no. I'll come and look." Hamilton's thinking, *who in the hell could it be?* He never swears, not even to himself. Hamilton nervously directs, "Well let's go see who it is." They both walk hurriedly, almost running over to the carriage house, and walk into the stall.

Hamilton looks and sees a large flowered hat covering the slumping woman's face. He slowly approaches with apprehension. Who could it be in his Bugatti? He can now see its Dedra, who smells of stale alcohol. He doesn't want Cleveland to know that he knows her romantically.

"I'll see if I can awake her, you can go and help your father," (who is two stalls away).

"Yessir. Let me know if you need help."

"I will. Thank you."

He softly whispers, "Dedra, Dee Dee, wake up. It's Hamilton." She moans and moans for a couple of minutes. Then answers, still slurring, "Ha— . . . Hamilton, I love you, you didn't visit me . . . me last night. I waited up until five a.m, then I started, started drinking my mother's gin . . . gin, then I came looking for you and I guess I ended up here . . . Where were you? I need you!" She is a mess like a sinking ship, listing and barely staying afloat.

Hamilton needs to take her home, but he does not need an inquisitive Rose or Emily next door seeing him do that. It's a small two-seat interior. "Well, just relax Dedra." *Hmm! Come up with a plan*, he thinks. *That's it. Ah! I'll lay her across my lap and throw a blanket over her. It is a little cool out this cloudy morning so no one will suspect a thing.* He slides her over to the right side. He looks for a blanket. Some are stacked up because they are still needed when the horses pull the carriage for transportation. He puts the blanket over her, and pushes the running automobile out of the stall. Slowly he drives away giving Cleveland Jr. and Cleveland Sr. a short, jerky, nervous wave. He makes his way past the massive mansions, then the Victorian cottages and into Dedra's driveway.

As she becomes alert, he feels her hot breath on his stomach. He tries to think of Emily and not become excited. He can hear her whispering, "Love me, love me, Hamilton." He thinks, *I cannot keep loving her lustfully. I'm giving her the wrong impression: that I actually have feelings for her.*

Hamilton pulls along the side of the house. His automobile is blocked from sight by a large tree and its overhanging elephant leaves. Dedra lifts up his shirt a little and kisses his lower chest. "Oh, Hamilton I could love and lie with you forever."

This is too deep, he thinks, *and I need to leave.*

"You need to go in and sleep for the day and I'll come see you tomorrow." She tries to kiss him as he pushes her upright. He steps out of the Bugatti, goes to the other side and helps her up. "Can you walk to the house?" He's not sure if anyone is still home.

"No! Help me in. My mother is at her tea club and thinks I'm still in bed sleeping." *That's a relief*, he thinks. *I'll just carry her in and leave.* He struggles step-by-step as he's not very strong due to his easy lifestyle. Up the side steps, he leans back and manages to open the door.

In they go. "Should I place you on the couch?"

"No, no, I need to sleep. Take me up to my room." It is a long and tiring climb. At last, he reaches her bedroom, gently setting her down on the bed. He hears some voices outside. Dedra's family is not wealthy, but they belong to the upper-middle class and do have a gardener.

"It's just Henry, the gardener, talking to the neighbor," she says.

"Oh! I best be going?" Hamilton states quickly, trying to hurry out of this very tempting situation.

"No, Hamilton, stay with me. I am lonely, all I have is my mother. My father died when I was eight. I need your attention, I need your love, I need you." She sits up and hugs him. Knowing her father is dead, he feels sorry for her. Hamilton is having the right emotion—sorrow. A great heartfelt emotion is what deems us to be human, although some animals exhibit the same quality. But for Hamilton, it seems to add to his reckless behavior.

He hugs her back. She kisses him on the ear; he feels her soft breaths. "I must go," he says, but he stays. She then touches him with her hand on the inside of his leg. His attempt to not get aroused is now futile. He is still thinking of Emily, which stimulates him even more. He can no longer resist this situation and moment. He moves his hands around her body, and pushes up her dress, finding her palace of pleasure. But soon after, he finds his own temple of guilt.

This keeps happening—the more he falls in love with Emily, the more satisfying these episodes with Dedra become. *What am I doing?* he questions himself. *I keep making the same mistake. It is like I am not in control, she is.*

"Hamilton, I knew you would love me again. I know you love me."

"Oh, Dedra, I must go!" Thinking of a lie, "I have to take Aunt Rose's dress patterns to her seamstress company, Peabody & Sons. I must go!"

"I look forward to seeing you again. Do I please you Hamilton?"

"Yes, you do, Dee Dee. But I have to go. Bye." He flies down the stairs, starts his automobile, and swiftly drives away as the gardener watches him leave. Hamilton thinks how physically pleasing Dedra is, but mentally he's impressed with Emily. Trying to sort the facts and the fantasies leaves some lost, and some found. Dedra's alcohol-laced kisses still scent his skin.

He arrives back at the mansion, and parks the horseless carriage. Rose is being carried down the stairs just as Hamilton comes through the front door.

"Hello, Hamilton," she instantly smells the alcohol. "Young man, have you been drinking? It's only eleven-thirty in the morning!"

"No, I was looking for a book in the library and accidentally knocked over a bottle of gin that Grandfather accidentally left out, and it spilled on my shirt sleeve.

"I hope it wasn't one of father's rare bottles from Scotland . . ."

"No, it wasn't."

"Well, okay. Make sure the staff cleans it up."

"Yes, Rose. I'll see you at two o'clock then."

Hamilton now sneaks into the library and finds a cheap bottle of gin and knocks it to the floor where it hits the bottom of the table and breaks. He pushes the button to summon the household staff who enter the library in short order and start the cleanup. He steps over to the breakfast room and begins to eat lunch. A thought of Emily, a bite, then a thought of Dedra, neither one escaping his mind for more than a few minutes at a time. Dedra is so physically pleasing, but Emily obviously is *sui generis*.

After a needed second bath. Hamilton returns to the side porch watching the activity next door. And watching for Emily. When he sees her walking with Herma and Erma, he strolls over.

"Hi, ladies," announcing his presence.

"Hello, Hamilton," answers Emily first.

"I can't wait to see you at the ball," says Hamilton, hinting he would like to see her sooner.

"I love your automobile, Hamilton. I watched you drive by this morning."

Hopefully she only saw me, Hamilton thinks. Quickly he adds, "Would you like to go for a ride?"

"Well, let me ask my aunt." She strolls back to the mansion and returns in a flash. "She said you're a likable and honorable young man, so if I'm back in an hour, it will be fine."

"I'll be right back," he says, and sprints to get the Bugatti.

Soon he's entering the Smith grounds where an eager Emily is waiting. They both are all-smiles. Hamilton gets out, runs around, and opens the automobile door for her. *A good impression is always a must*, he thinks.

"Where shall we go?" he asks.

"How about a ride along the ocean?"

"The ocean it is," he beamingly agrees.

With Dedra, Hamilton becomes very physical; but with Emily he must remain passive. So, he reaches over just to hold her hand. Well, maybe more. They take off and the air whips their hair into new shapes. Talking loud over the motor's noise, his hand moves a little too far.

"Hamilton, you are an aggressive young man."

"Oh, not usually but, I really like you M." She swiftly stops his moving hand. She wants his attention, but a lady controls her passion, so she's been taught. *The scenic drive with the ocean's splashing waves is a perfect backdrop for young love*, Hamilton thinks. He pulls off to the side of the road.

"You are a beautiful and glamorous young woman, Emily. I sincerely mean that."

"Oh my, Hamilton, are you trying to seduce or impress me?"

"Both. I mean, neither. I mean, I'm speaking from my heart."

"But you hardly know me . . ."

"Since I first saw you, I knew I wanted you."

"You want me? My real love? Or my deeply romantic love? Which do you desire, Hamilton?

"I want your unending love and I will wait for the rest . . ."

"I'm only sixteen. Surely you won't wait two years or more, will you?

"I will if I know you will. I will wait." How can he lie to her face? He hasn't even waited one month. He leans in to kiss her. She wants the kiss too, but turns her head and he kisses her cheek.

"I should return. I told my Aunt an hour only and we are fifteen minutes past that." She is filled with excitement, but maintains a calm outward appearance.

Hamilton doesn't need to drive the Bugatti home; he could float there with his elevated feelings. He takes Emily home and again opens the door for her departure.

"Thank you Hamilton."

"You're most welcome, it was my pleasure," Hamilton responds and drives away. Kissing Emily once gives more mental satisfaction than kissing Dedra over and over, and *all* over. His mind spins out of control, *then why do I lust after Dee Dee? When will I kiss M again?* Kisses for love, kisses for lust, his mind becomes a battleground of good and evil, his actions will declare the winner.

Chapter 11

Finally, the day of the jazz ball. This July morning is filled with joyous and zealous anticipation for the celebration of Emily's seventeenth birthday. Even the birds are singing more loudly and the squirrels are dancing across the lawn in playful precision throwing their bushy tails around.

Hamilton is up early, pacing around, looking at his evening outfit, *this suit that resembles a penguin's appearance.* Looking at his recent haircut, his fingernails, he stretches and flexes his arms in front of a mirror. *Will I look good enough? Am I smart enough to hold a conversation with Emily or the guests? Am I agile enough to dance well?* While next door Emily is up and talking and giggling with Herma and Erma. Their fitted gowns and dresses hang on a clothes bar just waiting for tonight's excitement.

The mansion is overflowing with activity. Extra workers are squeezed into the kitchen—cutting, boiling, cleaning, sorting, collecting, counting, preparing, steaming, and baking. They pour over each dish and choice of food. Stacks of bread, pastries, cookies, meats, fruits, and vegetables are piling high. The fruits and vegetables are being diced, sliced, and shaped.

All of this must be beyond great, as these guests are accustomed to, and expect, perfection. Rose is even out on her balcony, watching the workers carry freshly cut flowers in vases that are being placed on tables already covered by pressed linens.

The sun seems brighter and the day's temperature a little warmer. Enthusiasm is hard at work. Rose falls into a daydream where she is dancing with a well-dressed, unshaven man in his early forties. "Rose, I have traveled the world just to have this dance with you ... Fighting in bloody wars, swimming in shark-infested waters. But at last I'm here." Rose would sell her soul for this daydream, but she awakes and continues watching the activity next door.

Hamilton wants to go next door and give Emily the pearl necklace. *What if she won't accept it? Will she laugh? What if she thinks he's too serious or some crazy-in-love boy? I'll have to take that chance and be a man, he decides.* In his casual attire, he exits through the front door, out onto the driveway. He strides excitedly, and soon approaches Smith's front door. He knocks with the door's heavy gold lion. A staff member answers,
"Yes, may I help you?" she says curtly with her Swiss accent.
"Is M, I mean, Emily here."
"Of course she is here, we are preparing for her birthday and the jazz ball young man. Would you like a word with her?"
"Yes ... Yes."
"I will see if she is available. Your name sir?"
"Uh, Hamilton."
"Will she know what this is regarding?"
"Yes, she will."
"I will be back in a minute, young man." The girls are still in Erma's bedroom, primping and prepping, daydreaming and boy-talking. Herma asks Emily, "Do you think Hamilton will attend?" Giggling, she continues, "Do you want his dances or his romances?"
"I want his dances and maybe just a kiss this evening. If he's a gentleman down the road, he'll have my romances." They laugh and share a song they know. *I am the princess bride. I wear golden slippers, we have a chateau in France*, each singing a piece. The Swiss-accented woman interrupts them, forming the question more like an answer.
"Excuse me ... Emily, do you want me to send away a young man named Hamilton."
Emily is surprised. "He is here now? The dance is not until evening. We are all in our undergarments." The girls continue tee-heeing and giggling.
"He's downstairs asking for you."
"Tell him ... Oh, give me a few minutes to dress and I'll be down."
"I'll let him know." Herma and Erma start to sing-talk. "Emily ... has a lover ... she wants no other."
"I wonder what he wants. Is he not coming to the dance?" She dresses and walks downstairs. She's nearing the bottom of the staircase.
"Hello Emily, how are you? Happy birthday."
"Thank you! What is on your mind?" asking like there is something wrong.

"Oh! Everything is fine. I just have a gift for you."

"If you go into the Grand Room, you can leave your gift there with the others."

"Well, I thought you could use this one tonight?"

"Is it a gown or a dress?"

"No."

"Then how could I use it?"

"Well..." as he hands it to her. "Please open it and you'll see." She takes the professionally wrapped gift and opens it, revealing the precious and stunning petite pearl necklace.

"Oh! I cannot accept this. You're very thoughtful, but I just can't."

"I insist. Besides they wouldn't take it back anyway."

"Well...Oh...Hamilton." She gives him a short embrace. "Thank you! It will look splendid with my dress. I will see you this evening then!" She spins with a smile and heads back to the girls.

Hamilton is pleased with his exhibition of himself as a man. Emily comes back into the bedroom.

"Well, M, what did he want?" asks Erma. She flings the pearls onto the bed where the girls are sitting, and says "He gave me these pearls, girls. They're just beautiful and exquisite. He's a charming boy."

"He's full of desire for you," says Herma and adds, "It's obvious . . . but should you hold a summer relationship with him? You will be back in England come fall. Will you even see that boy again?"

"Oh, let me enjoy this day. The end of summer is more than a twelfth of the year away."

Now back home, Hamilton's smile looks permanent as he whistles around the mansion with his head full of Emily. As he dreams of kissing and touching her, his temperature increases. He thinks of this evening's dance, he is not a great dancer. He goes into the library and finds a book, *Modern Dance*. He must do a quick study. Some of these look familiar, some do not. What if Emily asks him for a particular dance and he doesn't know it? *I'll look like a flat tire*, he thinks.

Should he have a drink to relax a little prior to the dance? Grandfather has a special hidden drawer for the liquor, keeping it out of sight from guests and the authorities. Hamilton is not sure why the government enacted prohibition anyway. People still drink, but now it is done in secret and people are killed over its illegal use.

He wonders if his friend Hans Busch will be there. He hasn't seen him much this summer, as he is working out west in the family business. They have prospered from the mining of silver. Hamilton's family's railroad cars haul this precious cargo east. Hamilton takes the fifth of liquor and places it on the inside pocket of his jacket.

The many types of dances he is studying and the thoughts of Emily fill his mind, with Emily winning the time game, although Dedra is still a color in his youthful diamond-prismed mind. The uncontrollable thoughts of her awaken him physically. Although he lies to himself, saying each romantic encounter is going to be the last, the next time is always more satisfying. He is driving himself deeper into this two-girl relationship, *this Bermuda Triangle*. He is physically in love with one and mentally in love with the other. *How can this be?* His reckless conclusion is, when Emily becomes his physical lover, he won't need the relationship with Dedra. He'll have both with one girl. *Strange*, he thinks, *but then the world will be perfect.*

It is getting closer to jazz ball time, so he must get ready. Up the stairs he skips, and into his room. His tuxedo is pressed and looking like it's ready for a long night. He asked for a new bottle of cologne and it's sitting on top of his dresser. A manly scent named "Woodsman" smelling of musk and a type of tree needles. Hamilton read about it in a magazine and thought this occasion would be fitting for the new smell.

He lathers up some lotion for a straightedge razor shave, looking left and right in the mirror as if these glances at himself will improve his looks. He puts the white shirt on, then the pants, the jacket and skinny tie, and top hat. Thinking *this bird is complete and ready to . . . oh well, penguins can't fly*, but he is ready. He struts over to the dresser and splashes on a healthy amount of the cologne, thinking Emily will be impressed. *Just look at me.*

Chapter 12

He goes out into the hall and knocks on Rose's bedroom door.
"Yes?"
"It's Hamilton. I would like your opinion on how I look?"
"Okay, sure. Come in. Oh, young Hamilton looks all grown-up and very keen." Teasingly, she adds "He is a man about town even. Yes, you are a handsome man." "Thank you, Aunt Rose, I wish you were going."
"What is the point? I can't dance and that makes me sad."
"I understand."
"But I may watch from my balcony. I do enjoy the festive sounds of music and people celebrating. Go have some fun, Hamilton. Go dance and make some lasting memories."
"Thank you, Aunt Rose." He kisses her on the forehead and leaves.
Hamilton passes by a mirror and gives another look at his debonair self, adjusting his jacket, and pushing back a swath of hair. Young Hamilton bounds down the stairs with his newfound swagger, perhaps brought on by the tux, the anticipation of the ball, or the not-too-distant presence of Emily.
He almost forgets the corsage. He had one of the household staff make it, a last-minute item for impressing Emily. It is sitting on a table in the corner of the breakfast room. He carefully picks it up and the sweet smell drifts like a cloud to his nose. He confirms, *what a homerun idea, she will be pleased.*
He meanders out onto the side porch and his eyes take aim at the mansion next door which is alive with activity. He can hear the jazz band warming up, while expensive and exotic automobiles arrive. The well-dressed crowd of

invited guests fills the area by the mansion's grand entrance. Men, women, and adolescent children are walking, talking, looking, and laughing. Some guests with a smoke, a cigarette, or a cigar. Some of the women have hats, some do not. They all wait their turn in this lucky line that money *can* buy.

Hamilton decides to join this parade of the prestigious and makes his way off the porch and down the side entrance out onto the sidewalk. He is as confident as a new millionaire; his tailored tux gives him the appearance of one as well. His quickened walk turns to slow motion as he nears the crowd, trying to take it all in.

He steps to the end of the formed line, acknowledging the guest in front of him. "Good evening, Ma'am."

"It is a fine summer evening," the woman cheerfully says. "I am Countess Melavine Hendrich. This is my husband," she points by lowering her hand. "The Count Marshall P. Hendrich. We are from Vienna, friends of the Vandernes. That's where we're staying for the week. We just love Newport." Hamilton sees the Vandernes just ahead of them; he nods his head and smiles. He has met them before; *they are at the top of the mountain rich*, thinking to himself. *At one time the Vanderne family had more money then our government. Maybe they still do.*

The line slithers along slowly as the guests mingle with large talk. "My name is Hamilton Morgan Slate III," he proudly introduces himself. But thinking, *I am just rich, I am not royalty like these two.* The Countess is wearing a long sweeping gown, its glimmering gold color reflecting her status in society. It's banded by a silver neckline and silver upper-arm cuffs. Her neck is nearly covered by an ostentatious diamond-and-green-emerald necklace, and long white gloves complete her royal look. She is pushed up three inches by her custom-slippered shoes. "It is nice to make your acquaintance," she softly says in a gifted foreign accent.

Hamilton doesn't smoke cigarettes very often, but he is nervous and this is indeed a special occasion. He lights one up and draws the blue smoke into his lungs savoring its flavor, until he suddenly feels a little light-headed, so he extinguishes it with his foot. The line passes the stone-eagled entrance. Nearly inside he can see the grand entrance. The music is a little louder as are these hundreds of competing voices.

A short, suited, pot-bellied man asks for Hamilton's invitation. He hands it to him. All of the words, laughs, shouts, and whispers make little sense when heard all at once as Hamilton moves along. He squeezes his way through the crowd on his way to the Great Room. He can now see the room with its forty-foot ceiling, six Italian chandeliers, gilded walls, family-portrait paintings, and dozens of ornate carvings—depicting castle courtyards of Europe. Each section is done with exotic and rare woods from all over the world.

Hamilton walks slowly, smiling and changing his direction every few feet, trying to navigate through the overly crowded room. The Ballroom is just past the Great Room; he inches closer, nodding and smiling. He is trying to find Emily through this world of invited guests. Looking around, Hamilton thinks he sees Herma. Hopefully Emily is in that immediate area.

He holds his hand up a little and waves to her, trying not to look too obvious or too obnoxious. She gives a wave back and motions him to come over. He zigs and zags past dozens of conversations, some boasting, some toasting, some sighing, and some lying. Most of them seem faceless as he hurries over to Herma.

"Hello Herma," with a perky voice, "where's Emily"?

"I'm fine, Hamilton, thanks for asking," she quips, then laughs, "Oh, she's still upstairs putting on the final touches of the masterpiece called *herself*." Herma is certainly comedic, she makes many friends fast and they love to hear her funny stories, some fact, and some fiction.

"You look lovely Herma and appear five years older today. You are growing up fast."

"Not fast enough. I want to see the world for myself, not through these rich rose-colored glasses. I want to see how the poor live. I want to travel. I want to help those in need, for those are the riches I desire."

"You are truly compassionate to care about the less fortunate." He turns his head nearly all the way around as he sees Emily in the corner of the Great Room making her way over. He's never seen a more beautiful woman. She's flaunting a flapper dress and her look is fatal to Hamilton. He can no longer hold a conversation with Herma who's still passionately speaking of her dreams. Emily's dress is one of the shortest in the room; its progressive style excites even the unexcitable. She's wearing the petite pearls he purchased for her as a birthday present. She has a small round hat on with a lone peacock feather hovering over the top. Her short hair is styled in small wavy curls; she's supported by pointed small shoes.

Emily makes her way over. The closer she gets, the taller she becomes in Hamilton's mind, like a towering goddess from the heavens above. He feels her alluring presence both mentally and physically. The physical has to be toned down mentally, for the time being anyway. She reaches a wide-open-mouthed Hamilton, who is feasting his eyes on her and is nearly speechless.

"Good evening, Mr. Slate," she says with a formal flirt.

"H . . . H . . . Happy birthday M . . . Emily you look priceless. You're the most beautiful girl I've ever seen. I'm glad you're wearing the pearls".

"Indeed. I simply adore them."

"You look very handsome yourself. Have you eaten yet?" Hamilton isn't hungry, but thinking the food will be fit for a king says, "No, have you, M?" maintaining his politeness.

"Not yet! Let's go outside to the food tents." They talk, they flirt, and Hamilton almost forgets the corsage in his hand.

"Oh! This is for you." He smiles, she smiles, and she helps Hamilton's hands—which desire more—pin the corsage on her dress.

"They are lovely. You are very thoughtful."

"How has your day been so far?"

"It's been frantic and fun, but tonight will be bodacious." Hamilton takes his hand and gently touches her shoulder as they walk along. His mind touches her deeper, fantasizing and teasing his body.

Guests are gathered on the lawn, in and around the tents, eating the world of food laid out on these eight tables—hors d'oeuvres of lamb, beef, pork, game birds, trout, and caviar, along with countless side dishes. Fruits and jams on beds of crackers, cheese platters, fresh seafood lined in bowls of ice. Oyster plates, sliced fresh game, fresh meats showing design meets delicacy. Quail, pheasant, duck, and deer, all arranged perfectly, looking more like priceless art than food. They sample some of this fine-looking food.

"This is delicious," Hamilton says and takes another bite of the lamb. Emily only eats the appetizers, of the one-bite size.

"Would you like a drink, Emily?"

"I would."

He is thinking of the fifth in his pocket, she is thinking tea from India. "I brought some with me."

"Why, Hamilton, we have plenty of food and drink here."

"No, I mean liquor."

"Oh, are you trying to get me intoxicated so you can see more of me?"

"No, no. I just thought we could celebrate your birthday with a sip." Emily has had alcohol before, but this will be a long night in front of family, friends, and invited guests so she must maintain her appearance.

"Well I will share one little toast with you. Let's go over by the wall, next to your property, under that big tree."

They start to walk over, he holds out his hand and she takes hold. Hamilton fights off the urge of pleasure and self-indulgence; it takes all of his mental strength to do so. He will wait and remain a gentleman. They reach the tree and he pulls out the bottle, unscrewing the top.

"Happy birthday, Emily," he says and hands it to her.

She just breathes a sip, "That's strong Hamilton."

"It tastes harsh, alright, but it gives a good feeling." She passes it back to him and Hamilton downs the illegal liquid. Mentally breathing out fire, he agrees, "It is strong."

Emily suggests, "Well, let's get back to the festivities." M's mini-sip gave her the taste; Hamilton's larger one gave him the taste *and* the effect.

He is feeling on top of the world knowing life will be no finer than this moment, possibly for the rest of his life. He wants to freeze the moment, but their stroll soon reaches the roar of the lively guests as they near the mansion. It's a different world from the secretive drinking and hand-holding one they just left. The mansion's palatial-sized rear doors are open so they can see Erma with her two prized and groomed Afghan Hounds parading around.

"Hello, Erma," says Hamilton as he steps into the room with Emily next to him.

"Hello, Mr. Slate."

"What are your dog's names?"

"Lady Laverne and Lady Quintan."

"Do you have nicknames for them? Hamilton asks.

"Of course, I have several," Erma says with a touch of sarcasm.

A group of adult men are gathered by the billiard table in the adjoining room, smoking cigars and watching the other men play. The summer breeze continually carries the cloud of blue smoke outside. Hamilton sees that one of those men is Emily's uncle, the owner of this mansion, Oslo P. Smith, who is not here very often. He works hard to build and maintain his fortune. Hamilton's not sure how Oslo will react to his liking of Emily, so he keeps a safe distance from her. He sees Oslo walk out of the room and towards them. Hamilton gets more and more nervous as Oslo approaches.

"Why, Hamilton," he says with his monotone business like voice, "it's good to see you. I was telling the girls a few days ago how we played football when you and I were much younger. That was fun. Hans Busch was there and your father. I can't remember the other boys. That was nearly ten years and several million ago. Ha-ha, great memories. What is new in your life? Besides your liking of my niece, the girls tell me."

With a red face, Hamilton responds, "Well, I'm planning on attending Boston University this fall and my grandfather wants me to join the family business after that."

"You should. No one takes more pride in work than family members. Well, most of the time, that is. Take care!" He pats Hamilton on the back with a heavy hand and exits the room.

"Goodbye, sir," stammers Hamilton, as Oslo walks away.

Chapter 13

Now Hamilton steps closer to Emily as Oslo disappears into the crowd. He sees Hans come in and yells to him. Hans is wearing a black-and-tan tailored suit that looks more like an expensive hunting outfit.

"Hello, Hamilton."

"Good evening, Hans."

"This is the girl who is here from England, Emily," Hamilton declares and smiles wide.

"Oh yes, the birthday girl," Hans confirms. "Very nice to meet you. I know these two, Herma and Erma." The girls give him a brief smile. He reaches down, "How are the hounds," nearly touching one of the the dogs' head. The dog growls.

"He doesn't like to be touched by strangers," Erma says.

The three girls announce they have to go upstairs for something, leaving Hamilton and Hans standing there. "Well Hans, how has your summer been? I heard you were working out west in your family's business?"

"Yes, they have me recording in the log book all of the silver that comes out of the mines, ounce by ounce, pound by pound, as it's being put on the train cars. *Your* train cars to be precise," he adds.

"Not mine, my grandfather's. Well, mine someday, I hope. Hey, are you still training that hunting dog?"

"Yes, I think he's ready. I've been shooting around him. Luckily he's not startled by gunfire, and he's a great fetcher. I think he is a winner."

"Say, Grandfather mentioned the hunt. He said Mr. Cottsman from New York would also like to go."

"Great! So, is Emily your girlfriend? I see the way you look at her. She's more than beautiful," he says.

"Um, I do like her."

"Good to know, or my first dance would be with her, but I'll leave her to you. Besides I see Alexia Vanderne is here. She looks like a Greek goddess. I'll embarrass myself just talking about her. She's eighteen already, looking more like twenty-five, so womanly. Oh! I'm off to see that girl, I mean the *woman* of my dreams." His voice elevates from excitement. "Let me know the date of the hunt."

"Bye Hans, I will!"

Hamilton is left there in a hive of buzzing people and their incomprehensible chatter. He notices the girls coming back and the music is alive and precise. He would love to dance with M and impress her with his newfound knowledge of this American pastime.

"Uh, M . . . Emily, would you like . . . to . . ." he can't ask her yet, "go into the ballroom?"

"Yes, we would." The four of them and the two dogs walk like a winding river to the room of all rooms. It's nearly one-hundred-feet long and sixty-feet wide. There are a dozen chandeliers, lit wall sconces, mirrored wall panels, and the floor is so polished you can see your reflection in it. On one side is a solid row of windows facing the ocean affording cool summer breezes. There are crystal and silver bowls set up on side tables offering an array of exotic drinks, anything but alcohol. There must be almost a hundred people in this room alone.

The jazz band, comprised of four black men and two Cubans, are masters of this priceless and unique blend of music. The notes are timely and the energy is strong, their instruments seem to dance by themselves. Hamilton and the girls stand off to one side as the dancing has already begun. Hamilton stands and watches the dancers, then looks at Emily with his boyish smile, gathering his courage. He watches a couple of dances, then his excitement finally extinguishes his nervousness. With a man's voice and a red face, he looks at Emily again and asks, "Um, M . . . Emily, may I . . ." he reaches out his hand and picks up hers, giving the silky smooth hand a quick kiss, "have the privilege of dancing with you?"

Sounding like an English play cast member she says, "Shall we Cha-Cha or do the Charleston?"

"Lady's choice."

"We are young and energetic, let's do the Charleston," she says, and bops her head side to side. Hamilton extends his arm, placing her hand in his. "My Lady, shall we dance?"

"We shall." They step over to where the couples are dancing and enter this new world—the glitter, the glamour, the prestige, the chatter, the jewels, the gowns. They all have a place in this sea of opulence.

Hamilton steps fast with his whirling feet, trying not to laugh at himself.

"Hamilton, your Charleston looks more like a Cha-Cha. Let me show you the right way." They walk over to the edge of the dance floor. She shows him a few techniques and pulls him back to the floor.

Hamilton moves about slowly gaining more confidence with each corrected step. Emily heartens him with her approval, "Now you're on the trolley!" They kick and glide as Hamilton's and Emily's fairy tale comes to life; with a flip and a dip, a twist and a twirl, a smile and a flirt. The room seems to move with them as they float around effortlessly. Hamilton is energized by romantic thoughts, which, however, are much more physical.

This dance, he thinks, *is heavenly.* But he would love to touch and kiss her alone somewhere. The first dance becomes a second and a third. "Would you like to sit this one out, Emily?"

"Yes, this is exhausting. I need a drink." They stand by the side tables and share a drink. It is a combination of mangoes, kiwis, bananas, and oranges. The taste is refreshing and unique. More guests are pouring into the room. Hamilton can see his friend Hans talking into Alexia Vanderne's ear.

Two French silent-film stars are now here—Giblon Pemor and his mistress Lucsha Muiye. Her dress is also short, as is her hair. She was a risqué dancer before the start of silent films. Men's eyes follow her every move and they jump at the chance to have a conversation with her, especially when Giblon does his own flirtatious talk with some other more-than-willing women.

Hamilton sees Harold Cottsman talking to his father. Oh, no! He sees Dedra in the same corner. *What if she sees me,* he thinks. *She will run over here and spoil this priceless night forever. She'll ruin this blooming relationship with Emily. Oh no!* Hamilton eases in behind Emily. "M, I need some fresh air."

"Okay, there's an open door," she says, pointing to the side. Then Emily sees Dedra. "Oh, there is my new friend Dedra. I want to talk to her." Hamilton, to avoid this potential disaster, injects his verbal poison, trying to sabotage their friendship.

"Um, I am not sure if I would be friends with her, Emily. I heard her father drank himself to death. Bad blood there, I think."

"Oh, she seems so sweet and innocent. I am sure that bad-blood phenomenon is certainly fictitious. Would you like to join me?"

"Uh, no, I'm going out for some fresh air." Hamilton quickly walks out. This is the worst scenario possible. He takes out another cigarette and puffs hard and puffs again and again, feeling the rush of the nicotine, which makes him more nervous and unsure. He walks around pacing and puffing like a crazed scientist about to discover something new. Hamilton crawls up to one of the windows and slowly lifts his head up, revealing his face to the window and peers into the crowded room. He can barely see Emily talking to Dedra. They are smiling and pointing with their fingers and hands. A dancing couple blocks his view for a minute like a passing cloud and then he sees them again. It's been fifteen minutes. *What could they be talking about. Are they discussing him?*

He's a mental train wreck, and it feels like the weight of one is pressing on his body. *Maybe this is just a bad dream,* he hopes. But it isn't. Life is full of uncontrollable moments and this is one of them. There's nothing he can do, but watch and wait. They finally separate, Emily walks towards him and Dedra departs.

"Oh, that Dedra is so much fun. She was telling me about this local boy who is so physical with her and she just melts like ice when they are together. She had to go home early and help her mother."

"I wonder who it is?" asks a panicked Hamilton. She must not have said it was him or Emily wouldn't be next to him now.

"Oh, I didn't ask as I do not know many people here anyway."

"What else did she say about that local boy?"

"Oh, just the first time they ... you know ... and all of the romantic details, how he touched her here and there. She is very comical in the way she describes it." Emily is laughing as she speaks. Hamilton's heart sinks, *what if M ever let him and he took the identical approach, would she then know that he was Dedra's lover?* In his mind it just keeps getting worse.

"I also need some fresh air, Hamilton. Let's go over by the children's playhouse."

The playhouse, as they call it, is an architectural mini-masterpiece. It is one-and-a-half stories tall, with two bedrooms, a kitchen, dining area, and a living room, showcased by a columned front porch. It is as large as some houses, but has more mill work and intricate details than most houses.

They hold hands as they walk and talk. The sentences are short. Hamilton would love to set sail with her, but the love he feels for her, and knowing M won't partake in self-indulging pleasure, keeps the boat safely in the harbor. Emily opens the playhouse door and they step inside. It's a child's dream with appropriate-sized furniture, little tables and chairs, plates and silverware—probably real silver.

It's one place on the neighbor's property Hamilton has never seen. It's strictly for the girly girls. Hamilton looks around; it even has a working fireplace, which you can barely see from the reflections of the house and driveway lights. They leave the playhouse lights off. All of the furniture is too small for them so Emily sits down on a floor rug, and pulls Hamilton's hand down so he joins her.

"Oh, Emily, I need your kisses. I think about you and a moment alone like this every minute of every day." He leans in and kisses her while his hand touches the side of her face.

"You are a romance-filled young man. There's more to life than my kisses."

"I know, but I've never felt this way before."

"You'll say nearly anything and everything to have your desirous way with me. I know the games boys play, but I'll remain a virgin 'til I hear the sounds of wedding bells. Would you just lie with me? If that will please you ... then that's all."

"I can wait ... I just want to kiss your stomach?"

"Hamilton you just don't understand what 'No' actually means. Well, okay then, kiss me." An overly excited Hamilton moves his lips to her revealing stomach, she stops his moving hand with hers.

"Hamilton, I will lie with you semi-naked, if you promise not to advance beyond that."

Here goes the say-anything part. "I promise, M."

"This is against my better judgment," Emily adds as she slides her flapper dress higher. He's looking at this priceless gem. "One more thing, you can't touch me," she says, "only look."

"Now, that's not fair."

"Then I'll compromise. You can only kiss me north of my belly button."

Hamilton agrees. She leaves her dress on, but it's neck high as she removes her upper undergarment. Hamilton is staring at her like a hypnotized monkey, not taking his eyes off her perfectly rounded breasts.

"M, you are a goddess. Just look at you."

"I see myself daily. I'm no goddess." His desirous mouth moves across her luscious stomach and up to her newly uncovered breasts. *She smells like she tastes*, he thinks. His mind and body are on overload, one of them shows.

"That's enough, Hamilton, I don't want you to overheat. Let me lie behind you, with your shirt off," she says. The shirt flies off, quickly hitting the floor, almost before the words leave her mouth.

"Oh, M." She slides up behind him, pushing her naked breasts against his shirtless back. "Umm, M. I have died and gone to heaven. This is the best feeling that I have ever felt." He feels better than the after-feeling of Dedra, but now he's still aroused.

"We should get back as they will announce my birthday dance and I won't even be there. Erma, Herma, and Auntie will be highly suspicious."

They dress and exit the playhouse, playfully running and touching hands as the bended blades of grass pass beneath them. Flirting and laughing until reaching the side entrance of the ballroom.

Then they separate a little and tone down their playfulness. As they step into the elaborate room, they hear: "Everyone, raise your glass and toast this birthday celebration, for only once in her life, is she a girl *and* a woman. For now, Miss Emily Gloucester is officially seventeen years old." Their raised glasses and turned-toward-her faces toast and cheer as she makes her way across the polished hardwood floor. Just in the nick of time.

Hamilton stands by the entrance and looks on, thinking how it's Emily's best night ever, and it is also his. He is so in love with this girl, this woman. He steps back outside while the guests are still cheering Emily and takes another drink of his own cheer.

"Hey, Hamilton what are you doing?" he hears. *Oh no*, he thinks, trouble is upon him for the illegal use of this fire water. It's nearly dark where the voice is coming from.

"Relax," he hears, "it's me, Hans."

"Whew! You just frightened me to death. I thought I was caught taking a sip."

Hans laughs and says, "Let me join you. My father allows me to drink on special occasions and holidays." Hans tips his head and the bottle back, ingesting an effective amount.

"That is potent, whoa!" he hollers with a fiery voice. "Ah!! The poison of ancient gods," and takes another chug. He hands the bottle back to Hamilton, who has another drink. With their liquor-induced minds and bodies, they head back. A host of weaves and wobbles accompany them.

A stranger walks by them as they enter the room. "Wow! You boys need to cover that smell up," wisely instructs the gray-haired man in a gray suit with a white hat who stops them and quietly asks, "Say, would you have any of that water left in your bottle?"

Hamilton reluctantly says, "Yes," not knowing who the man is. "There is only a swig or two left." He suggests, "Let's step outside." They do and Hamilton hands the man the small amount that's left. "Much obliged!" the man says with a gentlemanly southern accent.

Hamilton returns once again to the ballroom and its reveling energy. He sees Emily talking to a young man. Jealousy sets in fast, like a winter's storm. He watches and watches, her head, his head, their facial and hand movements. *What are they saying? What are they doing?* Each second seems like a minute, he walks closer and sees its one of the Vanderne Boys, Isaac to be exact.

He mistrusts this boy. Isaac is only eighteen and already has a reputation of love-them-and-leave-them, a playboy, a gunslinger even. So many girls fall for his debonair style and graceful use of the right words and catch phrases. Isaac could melt a girl's heart made of stone, so some say. Hamilton must take her away from this presumed King of Love.

He heads over, gaining strength and composure with each step, like a professional lion tamer.

"Emily," he smiles and whispers in her ear, "can you go with me to the playhouse? I left something there."

"I will, but first . . ." she points. "Isaac wants me to do the Foxtrot."

Oh no! Hamilton thinks. *First the dance, then the romance.* It's an old saying that's bouncing like a ball through his head, over and over. Up and down, back and forth, until he feels intense mental pain. It could be the side effects of the alcohol, but at this moment it doesn't matter.

Hamilton's grimace is obvious to Emily. Isaac swiftly takes her hand leading M to his world of controlled charm. He firmly slows her down and speeds her up, showing off his knowledge of dance. Hamilton stands there lost in this moment of disbelief, hoping the King of Love will trip up and fall to the floor. But the foxtrot flows perfectly like a waterfall, giving satisfaction to those curious enough to watch, except for one.

The dance comes to an end, Isaac swirls her around again and positions her hand for a devious kiss. The sight is sickening to Hamilton, his heart is bruised. But, like a wounded warrior he maintains his position, waiting for Emily to return.

She waves goodbye to Isaac and glides over to Hamilton.

"Um, you're a good dancer. M, do you know that boy?"

"Know him! Of course I do." His heart sinks further. *Maybe she likes him and that's why she won't be totally romantic with me*, he thinks.

"How long have you known him?"

"Well, he was at my house in England three months ago."

"M, do you like him?"

"No," she says. "I actually *love* him." His face turns ashen. She senses his jealously.

"He's my cousin, you foolish boy." Hamilton lets out a loud sound of relief, resembling a donkey's hee-haw.

"Emily, I love you," he says and gives her a hug.

"Have you had more to drink? You're very emotional it seems."

"Just a little, but I gave the bottle to that man over there."

"Hamilton, do you know him?"

"No, do you?"

"Yes, Erma said that's Commodore Albert Sykes. He worked as a ship captain for years. Now he designs them. Brilliant thinkers do become rich, especially in America," she adds.

The birthday presents have piled up on one of the side tables. Emily says, "I must open all of these shortly or the givers will be disappointed without their deserved recognition."

She walks up to where the band is playing and they stop as she waves her hand down.

"Hello! Hello!" The crowd turns to her. "I wish to thank everyone for attending and celebrating my birthday with me. I shall be forever grateful to each one of you. Gifts I do not need, but, indeed I do want them. I shall open them all tomorrow, for tonight we shall enjoy the music." She waves her hand up like a cheer, steps away from the band, and the music leaps back into the air.

"Did you want to find what you lost in the playhouse, Hamilton?"

"Oh, I found it when you were dancing. I thought I lost my, um . . . pocket-watch," thinking hopefully that liars don't go too far into hell.

Chapter 14

He stands continuing to talk to her, as Erma and Herma come back along with the dogs.

"Hello, girls," Hamilton says.

"It's getting late and I wish to say good night," announces Erma. "Again, happy birthday, M. I hope your night was special."

"It was and is. There's a little of this night left. Good night then," she gives Erma an embrace.

Herma declares, "*I'm* staying up a little longer and going out to the tents for a taste delight. Will you join me?" They both say yes and follow her across the pampered lawn and around to the back of the mansion.

Some of the guests have gone, but there is a sizable crowd still left. Dozens of half-eaten plates line the tables, but plenty of scrumptious food remains. Neither duck livers nor the oysters appeal to Hamilton or the girls. Both are an acquired taste, usually consumed by *grown-ups*. The desserts consisting of custards, tarts, pies, and Emily's eight-layer chocolate birthday cake all look irresistible, but this evening, only the celebratory cake will do. Each of them takes a generous slice and places it on the French Limoge plates.

The evening of glitter, glamour, and fun is nearing its end. The remaining guests are now leaving; their chauffeurs are opening the doors of the expensive and exquisite automobiles—Duisenbergs, Fords, and the *French-* and *Italian-*made masterpieces with hard-to-pronounce names. There is one horse-drawn carriage mingled among them, perhaps as a show of nostalgia or the owner's reluctance to accept this modern age.

Herma finishes the cake and excuses herself for the evening. Hamilton and Emily stroll around the grounds of the mansion. Just being with her is satisfying to him mentally. However this night filled with her kisses, embraces, and touching leaves him physically excited. Repeatedly he has said he will wait, so he must. Besides, Emily won't give in to her own physical desires, let alone his.

They hold hands, kiss, and exchange sweet words for another hour, then it is time to end the evening.

"Oh, Emily, these have been the most memorable hours of my life, the *crème de la crème* of all evenings. I am so in love with you. I hope that this evening, along with me, have given you near-complete satisfaction."

"Hamilton, I couldn't have asked for an evening more special—your romantic charm, all of our dances, and conversation. It's been an excitingly perfect birthday. It all leaves me breathless. So I must say good night. Hamilton, I simply adore you!" she says and then kisses him firmly on the lips. Hamilton's lips are permanently fixed to hers, even as she says good night and walks towards the Oslo P. Smith mansion. His mind is holding the moment and he is perfectly still. Finally, her closing of the massive front door makes enough sound for him to de-trance.

He turns for home and whistles along the way. Hamilton is in his first love. *The other girls were mere stepping stones of romance, unlasting lessons of lust, and fleeting flirtations of flight*, he thinks. He walks slowly, absorbing these feel-good moments of love found.

Life could not be more pleasing. He shuffles along, reaching his own yard. It's late, the lights are dim, and he sits down at the front steps at the mansion. He's so physically excited about Emily. He starts thinking physically about Dedra. It is past midnight and the moon is near-full, lighting up the normally darkened sky. He thinks of Dedra and then Emily and then Dedra and Emily, back and forth. This totally excites him. He decides to take a self-gratifying, and self-defeating, walk in Dedra's direction. He won't go all the way to her house as that would be irresponsible and reckless. He can control his urges, and his love for Emily will put the brakes on these lustful feelings. He keeps thinking, trying to curb these physical stimulations.

The more he thinks, the worse it becomes. His body steers his mind like a boat through water. The closer he gets to Dedra's house, the more he loses his mental control. His thinking process is shutting down. With only one block to go, he can taste her on his lips; still he thinks he's in control and can stop this at anytime. His physical excitement becomes primal, like an uncontrollable addiction.

Hamilton stops in front of Dedra's house. It's late, thus the entire house is dark. He steps closer and moves down the tree-covered driveway. He has only been here once, but he remembers that Dedra's bedroom is in the back of the house. He steps past the front of this charming Victorian cottage, past the side entrance, and reaches the back.

This boy of a man, whose physical needs draw him in deeper to this dangerous and irresponsible romantic destination, is obviously out of control. He looks up at her second-storey bedroom window and the balcony under it. She'll think he is an intruder or a crazed robber, but his physical drive overrules.

He quickly studies the situation—there is a trellis attached to the house. He can climb that. He grabs hold and starts the climb. *It feels solid enough,* he thinks. He reaches the top and pulls himself over the railing and onto the balcony. He's so nervous and so excited that he's actually here and she's so near. He quietly slides up to the double doors and knocks with his fingers. He waits for a few seconds and knocks again. He hears steps from inside the room. It is a moonlit night so Dedra can see out. She thinks she recognizes the shadowy figure, and she hopes it's Hamilton. She walks over by the edge of the doors and whispers, "Hamilton, is that you?"

"Yes, yes, sorry to alarm you. I've been thinking about you and I can't sleep."

"Me, either," she says and opens the doors. "Go back down I will come down in a minute." Hamilton slides back down with the agility of a chimpanzee. He steps onto the ground and away from the house. He watches Dedra climb down; he watches all of her climb down. He stares at her body, watching each step and the figure of her that this full-moon night reveals. Dedra quickly walks up to him. Taking his hand, they walk away from the house toward the barn a hundred feet away.

"I have missed you Hamilton. I was at Emily's jazz ball earlier but lost interest in it promptly. I thought I woud see you there as you live next door? Did you go?"

"Yes, I went for a little while."

"Did you have fun?"

"Oh, it was fine, but it was not anything special," hoping this lie won't put him over heaven's acceptable level.

Dedra squeezes his hand as they travel the short distance. Hamilton squeezes hers back with his overly excited hand. He wants to ease her to the ground right here but she continues to lead him like a horse to water. She opens the door of the barn. The smell is of horses, who give startled sounds. She calls them by their names, Sir Windsor and Sir Cromwell. They calm down instantly with her familiar voice. She pulls Hamilton to her just inside of the door, "I am on fire for you, Hamilton." Her hands run up his back and around his neck. "I get so lonely for you during the daytime, that I imagine us together, all entangled so close together. It just melts me. I can't help myself. I wish you could be with me under my skin every minute." She unbuckles his pants and pulls him down to her where she is lying on blanket-covered bales of straw, just outside of the horse's stalls. He rolls her onto him. Hamilton is so intoxicated with her smell and her touch. He wants to open her night gown and reveal her naked skin so he pulls the gown apart and the buttons fly off one by one, like poker chips at the Newport Casino. Her breasts fall onto his chest bouncing softly like heavenly clouds.

"Oh, Hamilton, love me all over. Don't be afraid to please me."

He reaches down with his rapid hands and pulls off her last remaining piece of undergarment. She rolls him back over on top of her. He quickly enters her fire; the fireworks are mental and physical, followed by sounds of celebration.

"Oh, my Hamilton, I've never been so excited and so satisfied . . . Hold me close . . . you're my dream and I'm so lucky you're real. I hope I have your love as well."

"You are very special Dedra. I think about you a lot," his lie-count increases.

"You make me feel so good, Dedra." She does for these first five minutes, but how can he just abandon his feelings of love for Emily for a few minutes of deceitful pleasure. Does he have no shame, no feelings of guilt, no remorse? Or are humans just animals with the false pretense that they are not? He is still holding Dedra close, "Should you go back, Dee Dee?"

"No, it's okay. My mother could sleep through a blockbuster of bombs dropping."

"Well it's late," he says trying to leave the situation he put himself into.

"Yes, it is late . . . When will I see you again?"

"Well, um, I'm supposed to go hunting for quail I think this coming week or next, so right after that I assume."

"I can't wait to give you my physical love again, my mental love shall be yours until then." They dress and stand up. Dedra reaches out and gives him a long embrace and whispers in his ear, "I love you, Hamilton." He gives her a kiss on the lips, "Good night, Dee Dee, you're special." She senses that to mean something more.

They walk out of the barn and into the night, each giving up something, and each gaining something. One longs for love, the other lust; but with some relationships, the two shall never meet. Hamilton's old friends—pleasure and guilt—walk with him on the way home, each having their say, each one giving their closing argument in this trial of the heart. Hamilton falls into his bed after a day filled with Emily and Dedra. Thinking he can have it all.

Chapter 15

His wake-up call is a wind-driven rain dancing off the panes of glass. Its noise is both hypnotic and obnoxious. He is slow to get out of bed, thinking that these two girls give him the physical and mental love he needs and deserves. Life is nearly perfect but then, this can't last. Summer will soon be over. Emily will go back to England and Dedra will also leave, as will he. Then he will be alone without either one, his selfish, self-centered, and egotistical mind thinks.

He hears a knock on the door.

"Hamilton?"

"Yes?"

"It's Rose, how was the dance? I looked over a few times...a lot of people there."

"Oh, it was the best, Aunt Rose. I danced the *Charleston* and the *Cha-Cha* with Emily. The music, the people. Hans was there, it was a lot of fun."

"Are you going down for breakfast?"

"Yes, I'll be down in a few minutes."

"See you then"

He lies there for a few more minutes trying to focus on his life. Soon he'll be at Boston University. He wishes he could move this moment into a life with Emily, one that's mental and physical, one he hasn't known yet. *But how will she be physically? Mentally, she's mesmerizing, just her physical presence is provocative. He must get up,* he thinks. Breakfast and Rose's conversation will help to ease his troubled and overly active thoughts of love and lust. He splashes water onto his face and dresses.

The house is always alive with a flurry of activity. The household staff is cleaning the oriental carpets and the hardwood and marble floors, changing bed linens. Its thirty rooms offer an endless amount of work.

He should walk over and see Hans today as the hunt is next week and he did say he would let him know. This way he can also see the new hunting dog. Down he heads for breakfast with Rose.

It's a wet, gloomy day, good for nature's irrigation of lawns and flowers. Hamilton walks into the breakfast room where a worker is putting fresh flowers in a vase on the table where Rose is sitting.

"Hello again, Aunt Rose and good morning," he says to the worker, "A fine rainy day it is."

Rose replies, "It's God's watering-can at work." They laugh at the joke's simple truthfulness. "Tell me more about last night. What did Emily wear?"

"Well, she wore a very flattering flapper dress and a small hat with just one peacock feather in it. She had on the pearls I gave her . . . She looked like a beauty queen, a goddess, and a princess, all three combined into one perfect woman. I was the luckiest man there." Then his words strike like a cannonball of reality. *If that's what he thinks then why the Dedra desire?* Perhaps only he can answer that question.

"Did you meet anyone else of interest?"

"Yes, I did. The Count and Countess Heindrich, and Commodore Sykes. The Countess was truly the most glamorous woman there. Besides Emily, that is. She wore a gold-and-silver gown. It looked priceless." Hamilton gives Rose the details. He knows she wants to hear it all. His time is the only thing he can give her and it's a small price for seeing Rose smile.

The rain is nearly finished and the sun is breaking through the clouds. Far away a faint rainbow is visible.

"Another soul has just walked through the gates of heaven," Rose says as she looks at its mélange of colors.

"Do you need anything, Aunt Rose? I'm headed over to see Hans Busch."

"No, I don't, but thank you." Hamilton is excited about the upcoming hunt that Grandfather promised and the special new engraved gun. With all of the summer dances, gatherings, and events, this is the one, true all-male endeavor. It is early man at its best, the hunter, the gatherer, man-versus-nature, with an upper hand given to man and his gun. Hamilton decides to walk, as Hans's house is only a few houses away. He leaves Sea Cliff and begins the short journey.

Walking by Emily's, his eyes follow the grounds and the mansion, looking for his love, but there is no sight of her or the girls. He walks past it and the next sprawling granite mountain, just a mere mortal house to its owner. Hans's house is in sight; hopefully he's home. With the unsettled weather, there is a good chance he is.

His house is flanked by winged lions. It is a grand summer home made of white marble from Italy. It's truly a Renaissance-inspired beauty. The ten outdoor water fountains featuring cherubs, horses, lions, dolphins, and mermaids, all compete for your eye's attention. It has small fish ponds with exotic-flowered lilies and an array of trees, flowers, and shrubbery from America, and the rest of the world.

There is a horseless carriage parked in the front driveway. Hamilton is not sure what kind it is, but he knows it's not a Duisenberg or a Bugatti. It is the longest automobile he has ever seen. He travels down the long driveway, stopping by the gleaming metal searching for its name. Here it is: *Crossley*. Hamilton has never heard of that automobile maker. *It must be foreign,* he thinks.

He steps up to the massive front door that is carved wood with red-and-gold accents. He knocks with the heavy ram's head.

"Good afternoon, sir. May I help you," states an older French-accented woman who is dressed as if she's head of household.

"Yes, you may. Is Hans here?"

"Yes, he is," she is assuming he is referring to the younger Hans by Hamilton's youthful appearance. "Your name sir?"

"Hamilton."

"Wait here." A minute later she returns. "He's in the Great Room, please follow me, sir." This room is set up much differently than Hamilton's. Mounted animal heads fill the walls—deer, antelope, rhino, and many other fallen animals from around the world. Hans' family members are avid hunters. The men, that is.

Hans is looking at pictures and a map that are laying on a large table. "Hamilton, I was hoping you would stop by this week. Is the hunt set yet?"

"Yes, next Saturday. Be at my house at five a.m. You can ride with us. We'll be taking three automobiles. Speaking of autos, what is that parked out front?"

"My father just purchased that one. It's a 1928 Crossley Tourer. What a chromed masterpiece."

"Where's it from?"

"I think he said Australia. There were two workers out there all morning polishing it."

"What are you studying?"

"We are going to Africa for a big-game hunt in late April of next year." He points to the horned rhino hanging on the wall, "That is my uncle's prize two years ago. It weighed over a ton. What a kill, what an animal. We only hunt the horned ones for our collection. I guess if people needed meat they wouldn't care. We leave that for the tribesmen to eat."

"Oh, I can't wait for the quail hunt," Hamilton says, adding, "It's not much of an adventure for you though, Hans, after you kill one of those behemoths."

"It's the thrill of the hunt that excites me. Some are small, some are large, it does not matter. My heart races when I kill them. So it's the same. Just the bragging rights come from the big game, that is all. How many people are going next Saturday?"

"Well, let's see . . . Mr. Cottsman."

"Oh! I know him," says Hans. "Is he your stock broker too?"

"Yes, he is. Then there's . . . um . . . my father, Grandfather, Doctor Everhart for sure, maybe the banker." Hans asks if his uncle can go as well.

"Sure, we have two seats available, unless you want to drive."

"No we'll take those two," Hans says and asks, "How is Emily?"

"She is fine."

"Do I detect a love interest . . . or one of lust?" He laughs out loud.

Just her name starts the thinking wheels in motion and Dedra spins in there, too. Hamilton says, "The only real negative aspect is that she'll be gone in about a month back to England. And that's a world away."

"It's not that far nowadays, with smaller, quicker ships, and new flying planes being introduced every day. They're faster now and with longer flights."

"I wish she were staying here . . ."

"Oh, you'll just find another girl when she leaves anyway."

"I don't think so. I really like her."

"Have you seen all of her, Hamilton?"

Now suddenly with a red face, Hamilton confesses, "Um, not all of her, but enough to know I want to see the rest." They laugh like evil scientists.

"Oh, here are the photos we took the last time we were in Africa. The villagers here," he points, "guide us to the largest horned animals, and we pay them extra if it's a near-record kill. It's a spectacular sight when you see elephants, lions, zebras, and all of the other animals roaming around. Oh, you should go with us! It's a two-week journey."

"I would like to go, but I'll be in school then."

"Oh I forgot. I went to college for two years, that was enough. Now I work with, no, I work *for* Father. Work, work, work, morning to night." *He sounds like Grandfather*, Hamilton thinks. Oh how soon life will change, his carefree, do-as-you-please world will be replaced with responsibility. How tragic. Just another working man, taking all he can from the world around him. The thoughts consume and depress him for a moment.

"Well, I should be off, Hans. You have things to do. I'll see you next Saturday. Hey, where's your dog?"

"I have to keep him on the back porch. My parents don't like him running through the house. And they say he smells bad. Of course he smells bad, he's a hound. I don't mind it. I sneak him up to my room sometimes."

"Let's go have a look at him." They walk along past paintings, rare antique furniture, flower-filled vases, and over hand-painted rugs and out onto the porch. The dog hears them and lets out an earsplitting, full-mouthed howl.

"Easy boy, he's a friend."

"Wow, that's a beautiful dog, Hans." Spots of brown, black, and white are splashed across the coat of his medium-build dog. "What's his name?"

"Lucky!"

"Why do you call him that?"

"Well, the man that had him before me was training him to fetch in a pond when he was just a puppy and the dog went under. He had to dive into the ice-cold water and save him. After hearing that story I named him Lucky. Ha-ha!"

"Can he flush up some birds?"

"I think so, I've been training him since spring."

"We'll soon see. I'll see you next Saturday." Hamilton shakes his hand. "I'll walk out the back."

Chapter 16

Hamilton is excited about the hunt. He has only been out once, and found no thrill in the sport. But it was an unsuccessful endeavour. Now that Hans is going, it's like the band of brothers on a mission. It will be a fun adventure and will also take his tired mind off of the two girls for a short while. Hamilton arrives home, thinking it is a good day to read a book. *I'll go into the library and maybe read a book about hunting wildlife or fowl.*

He enters through the front door and trots into the book-filled room with renewed energy. He is focused and concentrating on the hunt. This adventure is a chance to form some lasting friendships and hopefully gain a much-needed closeness to his father and grandfather. *Besides it may be Grandfathers last hunt,* he thinks. But most importantly, he will be given that special gift—the gun.

He looks at the mountain of books lining the walnut shelves. Here is one titled *The First Hunt* by Peabody Blumfield. He picks it up and lets the pages fly with his fingers. Flip, flip, always stopping at the illustrated pages, one of which shows a hunting scene. An older boy is carrying a rabbit whose blood is dripping onto the snow. He flips to another page: "Safety first, know where your hunting group is at all times. If you're unsure, don't shoot, even at a prized animal." *Good advice,* he thinks, and reads on.

Hunting is exciting, but the thoughts of Emily and Dedra come crashing in like waves in a storm. Now that's real excitement, hand-sweating, pulse-pounding, so mentally and physically stimulating. How can hunting top that? But this hunt is just one weekend; love and lust, he thinks, will be a lifelong occurrence. He reads on: "Tips on cleaning guns", "Using sights for precision accuracy", "Different types of shotguns 8-, 10-, 12-, and 16-gauge", "How to field-dress an animal". He finds the sight of blood—his or someone else's—a little sickening.

Rose enters the room. "Hello, what are you reading? I didn't think that was something you did?" she jokingly asks.

"Normally I don't, but I thought I would do a quick study about hunting."

"Oh, yes, next weekend's fun for the men's club. If I could walk, I'd stir up the birds ahead of you, gun followers. If you eat them, then it's acceptable to hunt."

"Yes. Grandfather said they taste heavenly. Besides, there are millions of birds in the world. There's no cause for alarm in taking a few." Rose is overly sympathetic in her love of animals; perhaps it's a reflection of her own helplessness.

"I wonder if Father is taking his 1880 Remington shotgun? According to him, it's his *lucky rabbit's foot*.

"I have not heard which gun he's taking, but Father said they usually take three or four, just in case one jams. Hans is going with us and bringing his dog Lucky."

Rose is sarcastically encouraging, "Well it should be a good hunt. A lucky dog and a lucky gun, sounds like a recipe for success. Just don't take more birds than you can eat, that is all." Rose exits with a slight squeak on one wheel, which needs a squirt of oil, but she probably won't ask for help in correcting it.

Hamilton starts reading the book again; words turn to paragraphs, then pages. His mind tires of the book and he drifts off to Emily-land and some magical moments alone with her. He is next to her in bed, kissing her tenderly on the neck, then the ears, and the rest of her exposed skin, with every inch of her calling his name. If only dreamers and fools could bring thoughts to life, then solutions would precede problems.

He welcomes himself back to reality, with those words of wisdom. *It's just a dumb fantasy*, he thinks. The only physical romance he has had is with Dedra. Maybe he is just destined for her lust and love, but she doesn't mentally excite or melt him like Emily does. Maybe her physical love is an unreal expectation; it's probably all a gross waste of time and emotions. He must read on and not think about the girls.

"Safety items are an essential part of any hunt. Brightly colored vests and hats will keep you highly visible at all times. Remember, other hunters may be in the woods, besides your hunting party." He thinks he now knows enough to hunt safely and effectively. So he'll head back upstairs and pick out some clothes for this adventure.

In the book they also mention wearing long-sleeved shirts to prevent the brush from pricking through your skin and to protect your skin from those pesky biting insects. He looks through his neatly arranged clothes. *Here's a red cap and an orange shirt.* He launches them into his suitcase.

He keeps questioning in his mind if Grandfather will remember the birthday gift he mentioned. Hopefully he wasn't too intoxicated when he said it. *His very own gun, now that would be inspiring! Would he hunt more? Perhaps,* he thinks. The reading and thinking leave young Hamilton wanting a break to clear his mind.

He wonders if Emily is next door. So he walks down the hall to the guest bedroom and looks out the window. Erma is outside walking the dogs around the yard, but he can't see Emily. He flings open the window and yells, "Hello Erma, hello Erma!"

"Oh, it's a talking window," she replies. "I assume you want to speak with Emily."

"Yes, if she's not too busy. I just wanted to say hello."

"She is inside with Herma. I'll see if she is available." She disappears for a minute and Emily comes into view and takes her place. Like the changing of the palace guards, only for Hamilton this replacement guards his heart.

"Hamilton," she says, still not seeing him, she yells, "Hamilton!"

"Up here, M. How are you, young lady?"

Flirtatiously she says. "I am very well, will your arms reach this far and pull me into your heavenly castle?"

"You are very happy today, M!"

"I am happy to see you. I thought you'd be so involved with the upcoming hunt that I wouldn't see you until next week."

"Oh, I am excited about that, but you excite me more."

"Hamilton, with those words your transparency is evident."

He laughs. "Can I see you for a few minutes?"

"You may, but I'm giving the girls lessons about proper manners in social situations so I can only see you briefly."

"I'll be right over then," he says. She laughs and says, "Jump if you want to see me faster." Hamilton leaves the window with just the fading sound of her laughter. He flies down the stairs like the place is on fire, out the front door, onto the sidewalk, and into Oslo's yard.

He runs over to her, out of breath. "Slow down ... I do have a few minutes!" Hamilton likes her assertiveness. He gives her a kiss on the cheek as M's Aunt may be inside watching and he doesn't want to appear too aggressive. "Can we go out by the cliff, M?"

"Sure." Their smiles do most of the talking until they are a good distance away from the mansion. Hamilton reaches over and takes her hand, "I miss your warmth."

"Is that all you miss?"

"No, but I would like to miss one more thing."

"I won't succumb to your physical romantic desires or mine . . . So you shall not miss that. I will let you remain an honorable man, Hamilton." They continue and the ocean is now visible below them, with its unique scent, blended of salt, fish, and plant life. It is a most welcoming smell for the humans that lie on its beaches and build on its shores.

This is nearing dangerous ground for Hamilton as he has had many a moonlit night entangled with Dedra nearby on this path they call *Cliffwalk*. Hamilton's hand in Emily's shows and says *love* to him. However, he can't help but think about the naked truth of Dedra—no pun intended.

His thoughts of her awaken him physically. "Oh, I have really missed you, M. I think about the night of your birthday and the playhouse. I would give anything to just feel you again that way." His physically aroused condition is obvious.

"I can see that," she says, "but this horse shall remain free from your stable."

"Um, I didn't mean that much."

"Oh! It looks like you did." She enjoys his physicality and flirtatiousness, but she easily controls herself. If you've never had something, you'll obviously never miss it. The wanting-more feelings, she has felt, but the rest is unknown. She quickly changes direction. "Are you ready for the hunt?"

"Almost . . . I have my clothes packed. Grandfather said he was buying me a new gun, but he is older and if he forgets, it is okay!"

"Don't give yourself disappointment until you have to," she wisely says and adds, "Unpleasant and negative thoughts can consume your mind. Always think of the good things in life, like *me*!" she laughs.

"Can we sit here, M?"

"You can." He sits down just as a gust of wind comes up and Emily's dress is lifted into the air, revealing her delicate white undergarments below. Hamilton's eyes grow wide as Emily takes her hand and quickly pulls the dress back in place. "That eyeful should keep you company until I see you after the hunt."

"It will. That was indeed a pleasant visual treat. God likes me today."

"If that's God helping you, then, as they say, the Gods must be crazy." Hamilton stands back up and they share a few more laughs.

"I should go, Hamilton. The girls will be waiting."

"Okay," he leans in and gives her a long and memorable kiss. "I shall miss you every minute, M."

"I've given you a visual image to remember me by, more than I would have imagined." She kisses him back. "Take your time, Hamilton. I must go." She starts running back to the mansion.

Chapter 17

He thinks about the flying dress, and this place, *Cliffwalk*. There is something special here that's both mysterious and ironic, with M's flying dress and the numerous nude rendezvous with Dedra. *Perhaps it is the work of the devil*, Hamilton thinks. No it is just his overly active imagination coming to life; the flying up dress makes a point for the latter.

This latest episode leaves young Hamilton with a wide boyish smile, along with the desire to see the rest of Emily's womanly body. A quick mind along with near-perfect etiquette, and yes, her physical appearance, all add to this *love* and *quest*. *She is nearly perfect*, he thinks. Hamilton needs to stop thinking so much. He is now back at the mansion. The hunt, the hunt, the hunt, he manages to pull that back into his mind, stopping it's Emily obsession and fascination.

Hamilton will turn twenty-four in December, but his grandfather may not be alive then to share that day so this hunt with the gift of the gun will perhaps be that *special day*. He runs into Rose, who is wheeling through the Grand Hall and notices his beaming smile. "Did you discover gold in the backyard?"

"Something that is more precious, Aunt Rose. True love."

"You are not old enough to know the meaning, young man, but I sense it is as close to love as your young life has seen. Next year you'll be in, as you say, *true love* again."

"No, I don't want anyone but M."

"Ha-ha!" Rose laughs. "Time will be the judge. Your father asked me to have you go into the attic and bring those large backpacks down. He said there are three by the oval window that overlooks the ocean. Take them to the kitchen, the staff will fill them with some food for the trip. Father was in the basement this morning collecting his supplies and ammo."

"Were any of the boxes wrapped?"

Rose laughs. "Wrapped? This isn't Christmas. This is a hunt for the men—man against nature with an unfair advantage for man. Why would he wrap guns?" Then it occurs to her why he is asking. "Oh, your first gun. I didn't see that in his collection." Hamilton looks disappointed.

"Cheer up! Your birthday is not until December. Good luck on tomorrow's hunt. Be careful."

"Won't I see you before then?"

"No," she says. "I am having dinner tonight in town at that new restaurant La Cha Cha with my friends Emelia Dresbick and her husband Elward. You remember them? They own the clothing store downtown, *Dresbick's Haberdashery*."

"I am not sure if I have ever met them. Have fun and don't eat too much duck," inserting his own sense of humor knowing Rose refuses to eat the quacker. It has been a long time since Rose has been out of the house socially. *That is certainly an encouraging sign*, Hamilton thinks.

With the men going to Connecticut for the quail hunt, perhaps Rose wanted to have a little trip of her own. That makes sense.

"Oh, Hamilton, take it easy on the bobwhites."

"What is a Bob White?"

"You will soon find out." Rose has heard many hunting stories over the years and knows the bobwhite is the *King of Quails, the Gold Standard, the Taj Ma-Tail.*

Hamilton steps forward, leans down, and gives Rose a short embrace. She smiles. He then turns and makes his way upstairs. His excitement level increases with the anticipation of tomorrow's hunt. It's only four in the afternoon. All of this preparation leaves him exhausted. So he lies down on the bed, but he's not sleepy, just tired.

So his racing mind dreams of Emily's love and Dedra's lust. It would be a perfect world and solution if he could mold them into one, like potter's clay. Then he would have it all. He pictures them spinning around and forming as one. But who would he end up with? A sweet, sophisticated, pretty girl? Or an attention-starved seductive woman? The thoughts go round and round until he finally falls asleep. These thirty minutes leave him feeling well-rested.

It is time for dinner and off to the dining room he goes. Grandfather is already seated. "Hello, Hamilton, are you ready for tomorrow's adventure?"

"I can't wait."

"You have not seen the two-thousand acres your father and I purchased last spring?"

"No, Father offered to take me there the last time they went, but I was busy."

"Busy! With what, entertaining yourself by driving around that Bugatti or chasing another pretty girl? That's your busy? Oh, well!"

"Grandfather, tell me about the hunting lodge."

"It is certainly not a lodge. Only having four bedrooms and no running water or electricity. It's just a cabin. I had the household staff take some of the antlers and animal mounts we had here in the attic up to the cabin in May right after the snow cleared from the road. It now looks like we have owned it for years," he proudly describes, and adds, "It will be the best weekend of the year—cigars, drink, and poker. Three sins and three pleasures. Now that is the good life."

"What time do we leave in the morning?"

"Five or five-thirty is fine, It's about a two-hour drive." The staff has placed the serving platters of food on the table already, but the men are too involved in their conversation to even notice. Finally, Hamilton reaches over and begins to fill up his plate, as does Grandfather.

"Sure seems quiet without Rose here," Grandfather says and adds, "I can't remember a dinner without her here. It's been many years . . . but she needs to live a little. It's good for her soul."

"Grandfather, what's a Bob White?" Rose informed him of the joke. He laughs to himself and makes up a quick story.

"Oh, that's the caretaker of the cabin, Bob White."

"Now that makes sense. Rose told me to take it easy on him. Well, now I know." Grandfather turns his face to the side and chuckles to himself. Desserts land on the table at one end as the staff clears the half-eaten platters from the other.

With a couple of bites of cake down, Grandfather asks Hamilton, "Would you like an after-dinner drink?"

"No, thank you! Five o'clock comes fast. I'm headed to bed. I'll have one with you at the cabin!"

"Fair enough. Well, good night, then."

"Good night. See you at five, Grandfather." Hamilton II comes through the front door as Hamilton's feet land on the first step of the grand staircase. He spins around at the sound of the large wooden-door opening.

"Father, welcome home!" He has been away for two days on business. He steps down and shakes his hand, as their relationship is almost business-like.

"It is good to be home, Hamilton. It has been two days of meetings with bankers, lawyers, and businessman. Oh, the price you pay to be prosperous. The hunt will be a much-needed rest. Is your Grandfather still up?"

"Yes, he was headed for an after-dinner drink."

"Great, I'll join him. Good night, see you when the roosters crow, or is it just before?" Everyone seems in great spirits.

"Good night, Father."

He climbs the staircase alternating his thoughts with each step. The hunt, the girls, the hunt, Emily, the hunt, Dedra, the hunt, the girls. He reaches, then drops into his bed with his body instantly shutting his mind down, like a machine, giving him, as they say, baby sleep.

Chapter 18

"Hamilton! Hamilton! It's time to wake up," he hears a staff member calling him. "Yes, ma'am, I'm awake."

"Breakfast is already on the table sir."

"Okay!" Hamilton looks outside. *Even the sun is smart enough to still be sleeping*, he thinks. Walking over to the bath, he runs some water into his hands and throws it to his face. "Good morning," he says, and pulls his eyes open by raising his forehead, and hurriedly gets dressed.

When he nears the top of the staircase, he can hear all of the familiar voices—Mr. Cottsman, Harold that is, Dr. Everhart, Father, and Grandfather. He wonders if his friend Hans is here yet. As he is walking down the stairs, he hears a knock.

"Come in," he shouts. It is the bearded man who shared his drink at the ball. The Commodore is slurring his words like he found another bottle and drank it by himself.

"Fine day for some flying feathers, I say."

"Yes, sir it is," replies Hamilton.

Laughing loudly, the Commodore stutters, "Got any, uh, pickled, uh quail eggs, son?"

"Not yet, but hopefully very soon."

Hamilton needs to find Grandfather. The Commodore is in no condition to hunt. He can barely stand.

"Wait here sir!" Hamilton quickly makes his way to the kitchen where Grandfather is. He comes back with him, where now the Commodore is sitting on the grand staircase steps.

"Albert," Grandfather says.

"G . . . G . . . Good morning my . . . my friend. Let's hunt." He has already had a successful hunt, but the bottle he killed leaves him unfit for the next hunt.

Grandfather says, "I think for today, Albert, you should go back home and sleep. We'll let you know when the next hunt is planned."

"Ye— . . . Yes! It's been a la— . . . long night, up all night with Captain Peabody Baxley . . . and two fine women. I think they were fine." Hamilton and Grandfather each take an arm, and steer him out the front door. Grandfather waves to Albert's chauffeur (who luckily is still there). They help him into the luxury automobile and walk back into the mansion.

Another knock, "Come in." It's Hans's uncle, Breslin Busch.

"Morning. Hans will be right along, Lucky was out for his morning duty and ran off. He usually never goes too far." Grandfather and Breslin make their way to the breakfast room. Hamilton remains there standing by the door waiting for his friend. Knock, knock. He opens the door. Finally it's Hans, "I'll leave Lucky tied out here."

"I was worried when Breslin said Lucky ran off that you wouldn't be here in time. I need someone close to my age to talk to or this will be a very long weekend. Has Lucky ever hunted?"

"No, but he'll do fine. I cannot wait." The household staff starts to carry the gear out to the waiting automobiles. Cleveland Jr. is bringing up the last automobile. Hamilton is watching the staff carry the gear out, still no sign of the gun. He sees Cleveland walking by the automobiles, so he steps outside.

"Hey Cleveland, how is it going?"

"It goes good, sir. I wish you a rabbit's-foot luck on the hunt today."

"Thank you."

"Looks like a good bird dog there. What's his name?" Hamilton and Hans say "Lucky" at the same time.

"Have you ever hunted, Cleveland?" asks Hamilton.

"Yes sir, but we don't use the dogs. It just takes longer, that's all. Well, I'll be off. Gotta git to work sir," he purposely slangs his words, as it is his way of showing respect. "They are all gassed up for you, sir." Hamilton thinks it would be great if Cleveland could go with them, but Grandfather would never allow it. Cleveland walks away and heads for the carriage house.

Hamilton and Hans head back inside and find their way to the others who are eating and talking fast. "Grandfather, can I talk to you for a minute?"

"Yes," they step into the pantry. "What is on your mind, son?"

"Well, I thought it would be great if Cleveland could go on the hunt with us?"

"Why would you want to take an employee? Do we need help carrying the quail?"

"No, I just think he would enjoy it".

"Enjoy it? You want him to hunt with us while I'm paying him? You're far too generous with my money, son. Besides that, your father would never allow it!" He can see Hamilton really wants this, and it could be their first and last hunt together. "Damn! Damn! Well, I guess this once it would be okay. I'll tell your father I need Cleveland's help, as I don't feel well today and need help carrying my gear. Alright, go get him. I've got an old shotgun he can use."

"Thank you, Grandfather."

"Yes, yes ... You're welcome."

Hamilton runs out through the back door, towards the carriage house sprinting like an Olympic champion. He yells, "Cleveland, Cleveland, let's go." It alarms Cleveland.

"What is the matter, sir?"

"I have talked Grandfather into letting you go with us on the hunt."

"You serious?"

Sr. speaks up, "If they says you can go, then you got to go, go on now! You got a vest for him?"

"Yes, we have some extra gear." All three display their teeth as if they are in a photo contest. They hurry back to the mansion as it is almost time to hit the road for the long two-hour drive.

"You have to carry Grandfather's hunting gear, Cleveland. That way my Father won't object to you going with us."

"Fair enough, fair enough! This is real thoughtful of you, Hamilton."

They enter the breakfast room, where the men are done eating and are talking about this trip and the hunting days of old. "I pulled up and with one shot downed two birds," Grandfather says. How stories grow with time. Hamilton's father looks over at Hamilton and seems very puzzled as Cleveland is just standing next to Hamilton and is not working. He walks over, "Cleveland you can go back to work now. Thank you for bringing the automobiles around front." Grandfather speaks up.

"He is coming with us. I just don't feel very well today and he can carry my gear."

"Well, good enough then, let the trip begin. Who wants to ride with me?" he adds, "I have room for three."

"Son, I will ride with Harold and Dr. Everhart," Hamilton says. "Cleveland and I will ride with you, Father."

Hans speaks up, "I will go with Hamilton and Cleveland. Do we have room for Lucky? Lucky has to go if his namesake will do the hunt justice," Harold jokingly says.

Hamilton II says, "It is a long drive, so use the white porcelain, if you need to. We will depart in fifteen minutes."

Hamilton seems quiet . . . still no sign of the gun. *Oh well*, he thinks, *it's time to cheer up now that Cleveland and Hans are along for the ride*. It should be a fun adventure. Most of the men are standing in front of the mansion, with hunting stories still flying out of their mouths.

Dr. Everhart says, "It was the largest pheasant I had ever seen. It took flight and was so colorful. I stopped for a few seconds to admire this work of Mother Nature. The damn bird seemed to trick me with that display. So he got away, chalk up one for the birds." It was his excuse for not shooting. He likes to hunt with the others, but has yet to kill even one bird. His job is to help heal humans and it carries over to the rest of God's creatures. Though he thinks this is the year to pull the trigger and give himself that adrenaline rush of seeing an animal or bird fall dead to the ground. Giving man that supreme-master-of-the-universe feeling, but can he do it?

Breslin and Hans are the last ones out. "Let us put these headlights to the road, men," Hamilton II says. Just as they are entering their automobiles, another one comes speeding into the end of the driveway.

"Who the hell is this?" Grandfather angrily spurts out. It pulls in next to them. Hamilton looks disappointed after seeing it is that Vanderne boy, Isaac. He is M's cousin, but he is too wild and too crazy. Who needs someone like that to be around?

He steps out of the automobile and with a self-invitation says, "Hans informed me last week that you were going on the annual hunting trip and I am ready to go. It will give you another set of eyes so we can blast more of those dumb birds out of the sky."

"Do we have room for this boy?" asks Grandfather, hoping they don't.

"You don't need room, Grandpop, I am driving the *Blue Demon* pointing to his automobile. Hans you ride with me!" he adds, "but leave your dog where he is." Spare the rod, spoil the child fits to a tee. Hans gets out and climbs in the *Blue Demon*.

"One more time, are we ready?" asks a frustrated Hamilton II.

"Yes! Yes!" So they slowly move along the driveway.

You can hear Isaac revving his engine like he is lining up for a *concours* race. *He's both arrogant and irritating, but aren't all arrogant people?* Hamilton thinks.

Chapter 19

He would give anything to be with Emily at this moment, instead he is frustrated and mentally imprisoned by her cousin. But, he knows he cannot say anything without risking the loss of their relationship, as blood is thicker than water. *What a dumb, but appropriate cliché*, he thinks.

They pull out and on to the street. Just as they start to pull away from the mansion, Isaac comes flying around them, passing each one of them like he is the self-appointed winner of a soap box derby. His wide devil of a smile is as bright as his automobile's chrome. He pulls back in after passing them and is now the lead automobile, but he has no idea where they're headed so he pulls over and lets the rest pass him, then he quickly catches up.

Hans and Cleveland strike up a conversation about the negative and positive affects of WWI, how one stupid and careless event could trigger a war of such magnitude, destroying so many lives and so many buildings. On the positive side, though it's sad to say but true, a lot of companies made enormous profits, as some always benefit from supplying war's destructive weapons.

Hamilton's father speaks up. "I did not know you were so well-read, Cleveland."

"Thank you, sir! My father says 'Read, read, read everyday.'" Then the talk moves to automobiles, those of the future.

"Looks like oil stocks are a safe bet in this modern age," states Hamilton.

"You bet they are," agrees Father. "We have most of our money in the stock market. There are millions to be made right now. It is as sure as my winning hands of poker at the Newport Casino." They share a laugh.

Isaac falls behind and then races to catch up, showing off for all those who care enough to watch. Dr. Everhart, Grandfather, and Harold Cottsman in the second car are reflecting on days of old. "It was easier back then with the horses, no breakdowns, no getting stuck in the mud, no flat tires," Grandfather says proudly.

Harold adds, "Yes that is true, but it took a month of Sundays to get anywhere. Why, I remember going from New York to Boston before automobiles. It was so slow. It was such a waste of precious time. Now I have more of it to devote to making money for my clients."

"How is the market?" Grandfather asks.

"Oh! It is unbelievable, I recommended buying B & L railroad in April and it has gone up nearly one hundred percent. What a return, plus it pays a dividend," proudly says Harold.

"Did we buy?" Grandfather asks.

"Yes, your son bought ten thousand shares."

"That is great. There is hope for him yet, but I still do not think it is smart to put all of your eggs in one basket."

Harold says, "The stock market is safe. Look at the last thirty years, it has a proven track record."

"Well, it still makes me nervous," Grandfather says.

Back to the lead automobile, Hamilton's father is getting to know Cleveland better, and is not treating him so much like an employee anymore.

"Is your father still talking about retiring?"

"He would like to. Father is afraid the world will soon run out of fish to catch. So he hopes to do so by next year.

"He is too young to retire. How would he survive financially?"

"He has been saving a little, but it does take a lot. I think he is just plain tired. Some days he needs the gitty-up-go of a young horse." Laughter fills the air.

Cleveland's wit comes out after he feels comfortable talking with someone. Hamilton's father looks over at Hamilton sitting next to him in the front seat giving him a half-smile showing he also enjoys Cleveland's company.

"Well, Cleveland now that you've shown us you are wise, I suppose you will not be staying at the mansion long and working for us?"

"Oh, no, sir I can't afford college. No, sir. I will be right there in your carriage house, driving your fine automobiles. That is a good life for me, sir." Hamilton II likes those words, but cannot help but think what a complete waste of a brilliant person's mind, and time, it is. He would never be pleased with his life.

He could be a lawyer, a doctor, a businessman, or a scientist. Who knows, unless one is given the opportunity? Oh well, it is not his concern and there's nothing he can do about it. Or is there? He thinks about how Cleveland's father has been a valued employee for decades. Is it time for him to step up and show his gratitude?

Lucky starts barking and seems unsettled. "I think Lucky has to water the weeds, sir," Cleveland teases.

"My seats do not need his water. I will pull over," Hamilton II says with a laugh. They stop, open the door, and he goes running into the woods. Hans jumps out of the *Blue Demon* and follows him. A couple of minutes later, Hans has a hold of his collar and is leading Lucky back and says, "He still has some puppy left in him and he likes to wander off. Lots of good smells for him out here."

Back onto the road they go. It has been more than an hour since they left. Isaac soon pulls out to pass, but an oncoming automobile forces him back. The vehicle passes and out he comes again, speeding up on a straight way. He is flying by them one by one. A curve in the road is fast approaching. He only has Hamilton's automobile left to pass. Another oncoming vehicle is now visible. He speeds up and barely squeezes in. It is such a sharp turn his vehicle starts to slide as he hits the loose dirt on the side of the road. He overcorrects and the *Blue Demon* starts going the other way. He yells at Hans.

"Damn it... Hold on tight." He is totally out of control. They slide sideways off the road and into a ditch. The automobile rolls over, landing on its side, throwing Isaac out into a ditch of weedy, muddy water.

The others quickly stop, jump out, and yell, "Are you okay?" Hans is still in his seat, looking as pale as a ghost.

"I am okay. Go and find Isaac, I cannot see him." They run around by the ditch and there he is, all mud-covered looking like a *chocolate bunny*.

He is rolling out of the ditch, spitting up weeds and the muddy water, coughing and gagging.

"Wow, wow," he says. "That was the biggest thrill of my life. Wow!" Breslin asks if he is okay.

"Yes! I feel great!" Breslin clenches a fist, pulls it back, and hits Isaac on the side of his mouth. He goes flying back and lands on the ground.

"You scared the horsecrap out of us, you stupid kid. It's time you grew up. Now, we have to help you with the mess you created. I ought to hit you again, you punk," reprimands an angry Breslin. The blood is dripping down the side of Isaac's mouth.

"I am going to tell my father, and I will tell my lawyer."

"You can tell everyone and every newspaper in the whole damn world and I will tell them I know the world's biggest idiot," Breslin says.

Grandfather steps forward. "That is enough, the damage is done. Let's push him out."

They stand on the side of the damaged *Blue Demon* and rock it back and forth. Finally they flip it back over, onto its wheels. "I have a rope in my gear," says Breslin, who is still visibly upset and shaking his head in disgust.

It takes several tries to pull the automobile back onto the road. One fender is loose and nearly falling off. Breslin comes over. "You cannot drive it like that, it could fall off onto the road and damage someone else's automobile."

"I cannot leave the *Demon* here."

"Fine!" Breslin says. He picks up his foot and smashes it against the fender, causing it to fall off. He smiles as it hits the ground. "Alright, now pick it up. It is time to go."

The men look at each other in disbelief. Without Isaac looking, they laugh. "What a spoiled brat," Breslin adds.

Grandfather offers his solution. "He needs a good dose of the army. He would either come back a man, or come back in a coffin." Back onto the road they go.

This latest episode leaves them mostly silent. Dr. Everhart says to Harold, "Do you know Isaac's father?"

"Yes, he is one of my best clients." Looking at Grandfather, he corrects the statement.

"Not as good as you, Hamilton." Grandfather knows the Vandernes are the wealthiest family in America, and perhaps the world.

"I know I am not your wealthiest or best client," he continues. "Isaac's father is a good man, but needs to give that boy more attention. He buys him too much and the boy does not appreciate it. It is too bad because Isaac does have the potential to be a great man."

The driving is nearing its end as they are fast approaching the dirt road that leads to the cabin. Hamilton has spent the last leg of the trip thinking about Emily and Dedra, his good-and-evil dilemma, his right-and-wrong, his mental and physical pleasure, each taking up residence in his mind. They have all moved in, for better or worse.

Their moods have lifted and the hunt is now foremost in their minds. This is Hamilton's first organized hunt. He has hunted before, although unsuccessfully. It really never appealed to him.

Chapter 20

They slow down and now visible on the right-hand side of the road is a sign attached to two poles, overhanging a small dirt road. It reads "Feather Tail Lodge", signifying a grander place than Grandfather's "it's just a cabin" statement.

"This is it!" sounds off an excited Hamilton II, and adds "I can taste those breasts already. They are scrumptious. Mmm, mm!" The boys look at each other and smile, obviously thinking of other breasts.

He pulls onto the old dirt road and the others follow closely. You can feel each crater-sized hole as they bump along. "We need to get this road fixed soon," Hamilton's father says. They now can see the medium-sized lodge, above its second-storey balcony hangs antlers and animal heads.

It is certainly more than just a cabin. Just behind the lodge, an inviting little lake shimmers. *Perhaps if the quail hunt proves unsuccessful, it will offer up some fresh trout*, Hamilton thinks. His father pulls up close to the front door, Breslin pulls up behind him, then the rest.

Cleveland is very impressed and says, "Sure is a sweet place, sir."

"Thank you!" says Hamilton II and adds, "We bought it... Well, Father and I bought it sight unseen. Had to have it from the photos and its description".

Onto the porch walks a burly-bearded man. "Welcome gentlemen." He comes over and shakes Hamilton's father's hand. "Good to see you, sir, how was the trip?"

Without elaborating, he says. "It was fine." He looks at Hamilton. "I am Mr. White." *Now that makes perfect sense*, he thinks, remembering his conversation with Rose about Bob White. "Let me help you with that," Mr. White says.

Breslin is still standing next to his automobile and says, "Now, this is heaven—no crowds, no noise. Man and nature, one on one."

Grandfather interrupts with some sarcastic humor, "Would you like more paper for that novel?" They all laugh showing their good moods.

Isaac, still a little sheepish from the rollover, follows the others onto the porch. They step inside, entering a great room that has a moose head hanging over a cobblestone fireplace. This place is so much smaller than their mansion, Hamilton thinks. But, it does give one a great feeling, comparatively so. This minimalism is perhaps a mental and physical relief.

The large doors facing the lake are open. The fresh air pours into the space, forcing one to breathe slow and deep. Mr. White is bringing the hunting gear in. Grandfather and Hamilton II walk over to the side of the room pointing to a large map on the wall.

"I think this is the best place for quail. It was logged off a few years ago. There are ponds, some small streams, and a few meadows. I think it is perfect," Hamilton II recommends with assurance. "We can follow the old logging trails. We will try our luck there and if that is unsuccessful we can move over to section 16B right here," Hamilton II points.

Perhaps in an effort to entice himself to shoot some quail, Dr Everhart says, "Which one of us will bring back the most birds?" He continues, "Let us lay down some bets. Who wants in on this?" Breslin steps up first and throws a hundred-dollar bill down. Dr. Everhart joins him with a one-hundred-dollar bet, so does Grandfather, then Hamilton II. Isaac cannot suppress his usual cocky self. "I will place my bet against all of you and your one-hundred-dollar bets."

Breslin warns, "Now wait a minute, we do not want to embarrass you twice in one day."

Harold Cottsman speaks up in his defense, or maybe just to preserve a great client. "Say, let young Isaac place his bet against us. It will be a good lesson for him. In the world of finance, you can make a fortune or lose one. One can take a lifetime and the other, just a few minutes."

Breslin cynically inquires, "Well, do you have enough one hundred dollar bills to cover the bets?"

"That and more. I could cover a hundred bets if I wanted to!" He pulls out a fist-sized wad of cash, trying to impress the men. The men laugh. Breslin adds, "A fool and his money are soon parted and I will give you two guesses who the fool is. Are all the bets in? Who shall hold the money?"

"Ah, how about Mr. White," Grandfather says.

"Hold this while we are gone," Breslin hands Mr. White the cash.

Hamilton looks around at all of the guns stacked up by the right side of the fireplace and still doesn't see one for him. Grandfather sees him looking over at the guns and thinks now is as good a time as any. He looks over at Mr. White and gives him a nod. He exits out the front door, goes out onto the porch, and disappears. After several minutes Mr. White sticks his head back in the door and looks over at Grandfather who distracts Hamilton by saying, "Hey look at that large deer standing at the edge of the lake." They all run over to the open windows and peer out into the distance.

"I do not see it!" says Hamilton.

"Oh, yes it is right behind you!" Grandfather says loudly. Hamilton jumps out of his skin and spins around. Mr. White is holding the brand new gun. They all yell.

"Hamilton! Hamilton! Happy Birthday," he hands it to Hamilton, who reads the engraving: "Hamilton may you find success in hunting and life. Love, Grandfather." It is a priceless gun, sporting a burled olive stock along with silver and gold metal work.

Hamilton is lost in the moment. He has been wanting this for weeks, but now he is completely speechless. He looks at his grandfather and a couple of tears roll down his face. He walks over and gives him a hearty hug.

"I love you, Grandfather. I shall treasure this moment and the gun forever." The men yell and clap. Cleveland says, "You no longer have an excuse for not hunting."

Isaac, adding his usual sarcasm, says, "Okay, enough with all these sentimental moments and emotions. We have birds to bury."

Breslin again, "Do you even know how to hunt, Isaac?"

"I could even show you a few tricks there, Breslin." Breslin laughs, trying to control his obvious dislike for him.

"It is showtime, boys," Harold says with enthusiasm. Dr. Everhart walks over and picks up his gun. Grandfather jokingly says, "Do you want to load that, Doctor?" and then adds, "I have never seen you kill a bird. We need a good meal and we cannot eat air, so you need to let the feathers fly."

Reluctantly, and perhaps just for show, Dr. Everhart grabs a couple of shells from his gear and puts them in his pocket, and says, "I will load as soon as I reach the great outdoors."

Grandfather calls, "Cleveland I need your help, [maintaining his cover] I have an old gun," he points, "You can bring that one for yourself."

"I don't have a hundred dollars for the bet, though?"

"I will cover Cleveland's bet." He throws another one-hundred-dollar bill on the table and says, "Shall we go?"

Chapter 21

They step off of the porch, make their way across the rough lawn, and start down the small logging trail.

"Load up men," Breslin says. They turn to Dr. Everhart and watch him push a couple of shells in, somewhat convincing them, but not convincing himself. *It is just a bird*, he thinks. And besides, he eats meat daily that someone else kills so it is hypocritical to not take a bird or two when given the opportunity. The rest of them throw their shells in.

"Hey, where is Hans with the two dogs?" Breslin asks. Just as the words are finished rolling off his tongue, they hear one of the dogs bark.

Breslin seems to be in charge. "Let's split into two teams for better shooting and some competition. We will trade dogs halfway through the day just to be fair about it."

Hans comes running up with the two dogs, Lucky and Dodger—a black lab who has been on several successful hunts already. Mr. Bob White has trained him well. Maybe Lucky will prove worthy of his name as well. It looks like they are finally ready for the man-versus-nature contest.

Each man has a gun in his hand and a vest on their chest, the one-hundred-dollar-bill bets and the anticipation of flying feathers on their brains. Cleveland and Hans were picked to carry the backpacks, one full of gear, and the other left empty for the carrying of the *unlucky* quail.

Breslin demonstrates his leadership, "Let's select the teams—Lucky, Hans, Isaac, and Hamilton will be team number one. We need a name for them, "The Lucky Dogs". Ha-ha! The rest of us will be called "The Winners."

Isaac antagonizes, "If you lose, you'll be "The Whiners"!" Breslin seems amused by the joke and actually laughs, and says, "We will meet back here in two hours and switch dogs. If you get lost, fire a shot every fifteen minutes and we'll find you. Good luck."

The Lucky Dogs does seem like the underdogs, but Hans is a great shooter, not a marksman, but close. Breslin picked the teams and deliberately put Isaac on a team he thought would lose.

They start out slowly down the opposite logging trails. Within five minutes Lucky stops and points. They walk with their guns raised. Two birds come flying straight up. Isaac pulls up, bang-bang, missing twice. Hans fires and one bird drops. Hamilton fires and misses wide to the right.

Hans yells, "Son of a bitch boys, we got one." He is now all fired-up. He runs over and picks it up and throws it into a burlap bag, inside of his backpack. He adds, "Let's proceed, no time to waste."

Hamilton is about to be initiated. Breslin is sneaking through the woods carrying a dead chicken. He is getting closer and closer. Lucky stops and points, the guns point to the sky, then Breslin throws the chicken up. The men are all aware of the prank. Hamilton sees a flying bird and fires and the chicken falls. The group yells, "Good shot, Hamilton." He runs over and picks up the dead bird. They all laugh and chirp like chickens. Brack, brack, brack.

"Now you are a hunter," says Breslin as he walks out of the bush. "Nice shot," he continues. "You are an old dead-eye. Ha-ha!"

Hamilton is laughing as well, "If we are counting score, then I have one dead bird."

Breslin gives in, "We'll give you that."

Hamilton's thoughts of the girls have been replaced by the hunt, but the day is young. Breslin, still laughing, walks back down the trail to catch up to the others, who, by the sounds of gunshots, are in the lead. Still showing his mischievous grin, Breslin rejoins the group.

Grandfather asks, "Did Hamilton kill the dead chicken?"

"He sure did and with only one shot. Ha-ha! Sounds like you're having a good harvest over here!"

Hamilton II says, "We have three, one of which was downed by Dr. Everhart, we think."

"It was my shot," Dr. Everhart reluctantly says, "but now I'll have to eat the bird with a troubled conscience."

Breslin tells him, "When the taste of that bird hits your buds, you'll forget about your conscience."

"I suppose."

"What's the count?"

"Harold: one; Doctor: one; and I have one."

Grandfather answers, "Well, let's get to work." They signal Dodger to proceed. They can hear gunshots in the distance, BANG! BANG! followed by a WHOA!

"Damn, those kids are gonna beat us," Harold comments. Dodger walks slowly alongside a pile of decaying brush, then stops and points. Six birds take to the sky. BANG! BANG! Four fall like the heavens are raining quail. It's a feast of feathers.

"No way those kids will beat us now," Grandfather proudly boasts. The boys are also working fast. Isaac: one; Hamilton: two (counting the chicken); Hans: two. But ultimately, it's each man for himself.

Lucky quickly gets back to work. He zigzags, walking just inside a meadow. They lose sight of him as he jumps into the thick brush. Silence. They hear the thrashing of wings as two birds come up. The three boys take aim. Isaac jumps up on a dead log for a better shot. With his finger on the trigger, he pulls up to shoot, but he trips. As Isaac is falling, the shot goes off, striking Hans in the shoulder, sending Hans reeling to the ground in pain.

"You stupid son of a bitch. You shot me." Hans reaches over and holds his hand on the wounded area and can see that blood is coming through his shirt. His loud, agonizing screams are heard by the other men. Breslin yells to his group, "What in the hell's going on!?" He begins to run in the direction of the screams and within a couple of minutes, he's there.

Isaac and Hamilton are trying to help Hans, who is as white as a ghost. Hamilton's subtle facial expression indicates that Isaac is responsible. Breslin angrily growls, "I knew we should have left you back there in the ditch, you irresponsible bastard. Get out of the way."

The other men are now there. Dr. Everhart walks over and rips off part of Hans's shirt. "Grab me a short stick." Hamilton hands him one, from which he makes a tourniquet.

"He'll be fine, I just need to disinfect the wound."

Breslin moans, "Well, this day is ruined."

"I didn't mean it. My foot slipped off the log!" Isaac tries to defend himself.

"You had your finger on the trigger when you jumped on a slippery log. You're dumber than I thought," Breslin continues to growl.

"Let's head back to the cabin," Hamilton mumbles, extremely worried about Hans.

"Can you walk okay?" asks Dr. Everhart.

"I can, but I feel very dizzy."

"Take your time."

Cleveland looks over at Isaac with obvious disgust and says, "We should leave him here in the woods for the squirrels to enjoy 'cause this boy is nuts."

Breslin laughs, "I like this guy." A few of the men laugh at Cleveland's humor, but they hurriedly return to helping the wounded Hans who is wearing his pain on his face. He grimaces with nearly every step.

"I have some pain pills and antiseptic in my bag back at the cabin."

Hans whimpers, "I just can't walk that far, I'm sorry."

Harold thinks out loud, "Let's make him a stretcher. Hey there's a couple of long branches. He bends down and picks them up. We need some small branches to lay sideways across these. We'll tie it together with vines. Isaac, let me have your vest." He lays the vest on the newly arranged stretcher. "This will work if we proceed slowly. Hans, who's sitting on the ground, gently rolls over onto the homemade contraption, with Harold's and the Doctor's assistance.

"Three on each side," yells Breslin. The six men carefully lift him up.

"Wow! Talk about feeling helpless," Hans says.

"Just relax," Grandfather wisely consoles.

"Yell if you feel worse," Breslin adds.

Step by step, rut by rut, hill by hill, the men are proving their strength. The sweat is dripping off all six foreheads and slightly running into their eyes. They've gone approximately one thousand feet.

"I need a rest," Hamilton II announces.

"Me, too," Harold seconds the idea. They set Hans down on the logging trail.

Grandfather laments, "I'd like to help you carry him, but unfortunately those days are over. My grain of sand is nearly finished," Grandfather refers to the biblical idea that one's life is a grain of sand, and a beach full of sand represents eternity.

"Are we ready again?" Breslin commands. They lift him and continue down the logging road. Grandfather is helping by keeping track of the two dogs. "Come on boys," as he coaches them along. It's slow-going, the unloaded guns are laying between Hans's legs since there is no one left to carry them.

This accident entirely changes the *good time* that was anticipated. It's a shame, especially as this is Hamilton's first real hunt. But Hamilton is not thinking about himself, or even his love and lust interests; his concern is for his friend Hans.

Chapter 22

Finally the cabin is in sight as they start down the final steep hill. Hans hasn't spoken since he was first put on the stretcher.

"We're almost there," Breslin says with relief.

"That was a long quarter of a mile," adds Harold. The rough grass by the cabin is now under their feet.

"Be careful going up onto the porch," Grandfather advises.

"Steady men," Hamilton II says and then yells for Mr. White, who runs out and holds open the door.

"What happened? What happened?" he inquires nervously.

Breslin answers, "Carelessness is what happened," as he looks across at Isaac.

"Set him down," Dr. Everhart directs. "Mr. White, get my medical bag. It's over by the fireplace." Mr. White brings it to him. "Boil up some water." Dr. Everhart reaches in and grabs a scalpel and a pair of surgical tweezers.

"Christ," Hans laments.

"This is gonna be a little painful, son," advises Dr. Everhart.

Breslin recommends, "Do what they did in the Civil War and down a fifth of whiskey."

Doctor agrees, "That might work. I do have some pain pills, but they'll take a couple of hours to work and these pellets have to come out now."

Grandfather had disappeared, and now reappears with a bottle from his secret stash. "Drink up!"

Hans is still on the floor lying on the stretcher. "We need to put him on the bed," Doctor points to the closest bedroom. Again they lift Hans and carry him, setting him on the small bed.

Doctor asks, "How are you feeling?"

"Terrible, but the whiskey should help. Wow! That's good fire water!" as each sip burns from Hans's throat all the way to his stomach. His face is beginning to turn red—certainly a good sign he's feelings the effects of the illegal drink.

Mr. White brings the boiling water in along with several hand towels. Dr. Everhart begins to soak the towels in the boiling water, and his instruments are lined up on the bed next to Hans, who looks both happy (whiskey) and afraid (wound). Doctor picks up his scalpel; Hans's eyes widen as the happy disappears from his face.

Grandfather comes in to distract Hans, "We put Lucky out in the woodshed so don't worry about him."

"Thank . . ." as the scalpel hits his skin, "You-ow-ow!" Doctor takes the tweezers and starts to pluck the pellets out, "Hold on, son." Hans's face resembles the frozen human face that was found in a block of ice from thousands of years ago. They both have that I-died-a-gruesome-death look. Doctor throws the second pellet into a hand towel, "We're almost done," he says with a calming reassurance to a silent Hans. Another one lands and another, after six pellets are plucked from Hans, Doctor announces, "You are a brave young man and you are now free of metal." Hans quietly says, "Thank you," as he tries to get comfortable on the bed. Dr. Everhart instructs, "We can leave him alone for a few minutes. He needs to rest." He collects the surgical tools and the towels with the pellets.

The men gather in the Great Room, while Isaac is still outside pacing around, actually looking worried. Breslin notices, "Look at him out there—careless is like careless does. Now we're all paying the price. At least we landed a few birds, barely enough for a meal, though."

Hamilton asks, "Should we take Hans home?"

Doctor replies, "No, let him rest today. He'll be fine, the pain will last a week or so, and he'll have some scarring. He's lucky it missed his face, especially his eyes." Isaac walks back in. "How is he Doc?"

"In pain, but he will be okay."

"Is there anything I can do to help?"

Breslin snaps, "Yes, you can leave and promise me I'll never have to see you again."

"I AM TRULY SORRY, BRESLIN!"

"Well, son, you might want to think before you act. Let this be a life lesson to you. You could have blinded him." The men look at Isaac who has a couple of tears in his eyes, finally showing some remorse for his carelessness. He walks back outside.

Grandfather says, "I think for once in his life, he's showing some concern for his reckless actions. Hopefully he just grew into a more responsible man."

Doctor thinks out loud, "I'd better check on the patient." He walks in the bedroom, and notices the pain pills have worked, for Hans is sleeping like a newborn.

Grandfather tells Hamilton to get the bobwhites and put them in the kitchen. Hamilton looks a little confused, but walks outside, "Hey Mr. White, Grandfather wants you in the kitchen."

"Okay, son," Mr. White steps into the cabin and asks, "Sir, you wanted to see me in the kitchen?"

"No. I wanted the birds. You need to clean them and start cooking."

"Oh!" he heads back outside. "Hamilton, he wanted the *bobwhites*!"

"Well, aren't you Bob White?"

"No, my name is not Bob. He wanted the birds. They are the *bobwhites*," he's laughing out loud. Hamilton turns red in the face and helps bring them to the kitchen.

Hamilton wants this day to be over, as do the rest of the men, but none more so than Hans. The delectable aroma of the cooking birds is making its way through the cabin, along with the fragrant smells of the other dishes. "Mmmm!" Breslin is licking his lips. Grandfather seconds it, "Mmm, mm!"

Dr. Everhart chirps up, "Well, one of those birds will taste bittersweet," referring to his troubled conscience. Cleveland tries to comfort him, "Don't feel bad sir, we all got to eat and besides God put those birds on this earth for us humans. We're just at the top of the food chain that's all." Breslin jokingly disagrees, "I'm sure sharks, whales, and bears would disagree with that." Cleveland comes back with, "Not if I'm carrying a gun they won't." They share a much-needed laugh!

Mr. White comes in, "Gentlemen, you can take your places in the dining room." They quickly gather around the long wooden table with its carved chairs, a grand hunting-scene chandelier hangs above them. Cleveland enthusiastically pronounces, "This is the finest place to eat I've ever experienced, sir," looking at Grandfather. "Thank you son, it is a pleasant place."

"Isaac should have *your* mannerisms," Harold says, giving Cleveland a compliment and Isaac an insult. Isaac is still outside sitting in his automobile. Dr. Everhart wonders, "Do you think Isaac has learned his lesson?"

"God only knows with that one," Breslin responds.

Grandfather states, "Well it's time to eat. Someone go and tell him to join us."

"I'll go," offers Hamilton, perhaps feeling sorry for Isaac. "Isaac, the men said it's time to eat and they want you to join us."

"They do?"

"Yep."

Hamilton and Isaac enter as the birds are being placed on the table. With wide eyes and ready forks, they pass the plates and each takes their stab, landing one of the cooked birds. Grandfather asserts, "Let's say a prayer." Breslin jokingly offers the prayer, "Yes, I have one! *'Here's the meat, let's eat, Good bye little bobwhite, you're a sweet and tasty delight!'* Ha-ha!" Hamilton II lightheartedly agrees, "That will do."

The men bury their forks into the perfectly cooked birds. The tasty bites are little bits of heaven, each one as good as the next. They nearly finish the birds before trying the accompanying dishes of carrots, potatoes, gravy, and relish.

"If this isn't heaven, send me to hell," chimes Grandfather. "Who's up for a game of poker?" he adds.

Breslin enthusiastically responds, "I'm in and the winner can take home the quail bet money," since the hunt's abrupt ending provided no winner.

"Great idea!" they all agree. Isaac only nods. He hasn't spoken a word in hours, which is certainly comforting to the men. They finish eating and Grandfather asks who wants dessert. Cleveland cheerfully says, "I would love a slice of pie, sir, if you have one."

"No, son! I mean real dessert. Whiskey and cigars, a grown man's dessert."

"Yes, sir, I've had whiskey before, and it had *me* the whole next day." They laugh at Cleveland's wit.

"Slow and steady is the key," Grandfather advises.

Breslin again licks his lips and says, "Ah, poker, whiskey, and cigars. Let's get started."

They stand up and return to the Great Room. Dr. Everhart informs them, "I'm going to check on Hans. It's been a couple of hours since I pulled the pellets out."

Hamilton agrees, "I'll go with you." Isaac looks over as if he'd like to check on him, too. Instead he follows the men, to partake in their pleasures of the body and mind. Hamilton II looks at Grandfather, then walks outside, and a minute later comes back in, carrying a couple bottles of whiskey. Grandfather reaches into a cabinet and pulls out a box of cigars. Breslin asks where the cards and poker chips are.

"Top shelf in that sideboard," Grandfather points.

"Who's in?" Breslin asks.

"I think everyone but Hans," Harold says. Breslin was hoping Isaac would not participate as he looks over at him, but avoiding his eye contact, Isaac looks the other way.

"What'll it be, gentlemen?" an in-charge Breslin asks, "Straight Poker or Deuces Wild?" He quickly answers his own question, "With these young faces around, we'll stick to Straight Poker. I like to play fair."

"How much a hand?" Grandfather inquires.

Harold answers, "One dollar and one dollar raises."

Grandfather starts, "I'll deal first and we'll pass the deck to the right for the next hand." Around the table they sit—Grandfather, Harold, Breslin, Isaac, Hamilton, Cleveland, and Dr. Everhart. Hamilton II sits this hand out, while he sips his glass of whiskey.

Grandfather shuffles up the deck, he throws down a card to Harold, who checks it. Ace of Hearts, his heart pounds with joy. Breslin—10 of Spades, *so-so*, he thinks. Isaac—3 of Hearts, *I deserve this today*. Hamilton—8 of Spades, *not great*. Cleveland—Queen of Spades, *good enough*, he thinks. Doctor—9 of Hearts, *it's just a game*. Grandfather deals himself a 2 of Hearts, and on again to Harold and around and around until each has their five cards.

Harold is first to collect his hand—two Aces, two Queens and a 9; two pair. *This is decent*, he hopes.

Breslin has three 10's, a 2, and a 5; three of a kind. *Great*, he thinks.

For Isaac, all five cards are different. *Bad hand, bad day*.

Hamilton has three 8's, a 2, and a 4. *Okay!*

Cleveland gets lucky with four 8's. *Winner winner*, he hopes.

Dr. Everhart is dealt three 5's and two 2's; full house. *Good chance the pot is mine*.

The last hand is Grandfather—two 4's, two Queens, and one Ace. *Two pair, okay*.

The men look at each other and lay their cards down. As they call out their hands, all eyes turn to Cleveland's lucky four-of-a-kind—his grin takes up his whole face.

"Thank you." Grandfather slides the pile, all seven dollars, over to him.

"I'll give you back the dollar you put in for me, sir," he offers to Grandfather.

"No son, it's all yours. Save it and put it away for one of your dreams."

"Or a rainy day," Breslin adds. "Life is full of those. Like today."

Harold deals next. Grandfather takes the hand. Two drinks later, Hamilton II joins in; he takes his first hand. Lucky? Or under the direction of his consumed whiskey? Cleveland, Isaac, and Hamilton have been drinking the whiskey slowly, but even then, it creeps into your mind and body. Isaac wins a hand, then Cleveland again, who's up eleven dollars. Two hours and four tall drinks later, with their flushed faces and a few card-dealt flushes, the men are getting tired, or drunk, or both.

Isaac decides, "Well, I need to get some shl . . . slee . . . sleep." With those slurred words, he gets up from the table. "Ga . . . nigh . . . gentlemen." He stumbles to the stairs and loudly makes his way up to the bedroom. You can hear him knock something over. The men laugh. Grandfather, Hamilton II, and Breslin could drink even more, but their experience accounts for them *holding their whiskey.*

This American game of poker took off like wild fire, around the time of the American Civil War. Many versions of the game came from that era. Two more hands are dealt—Breslin takes both pots. Hamilton says good night next, then Cleveland, both appear beyond *a little tipsy.*

"Well, gentlemen," Grandfather says, "It's been a long day."

Breslin and Hamilton II coax, "C'mon, just one more."

Harold agrees with Grandfather, "I too have had enough cards and whiskey," his voice and actions reflecting both.

Breslin referees, "We'll have to call it quits then, just when I couldn't lose! Damn!"

They all say good night with their heads and bodies swaying as they make their way to the beds. Hamilton and Cleveland find theirs spinning like a merry-go-round. Hamilton tries to stop the motion by placing one foot on the floor. Soon, but not soon enough, he is fast asleep.

Chapter 23

Morning comes too soon for most of the men, with the smells of breakfast making their way through the cabin. But this morning, the smell of food gives them a queasy feeling. One that is too uncontrollable for Cleveland, who runs down the stairs out onto the porch and lets go of last night's food and drink. Mr. White is outside, bringing in wood for the cook stove.

Cleveland chokes, "Same thing happened the last time. Whiskey feels like heaven going in and hell coming out." Mr. White laughs and continues placing wood in his arms.

"Only thing that helps is sleep, son," he advises.

Cleveland agrees. "I am headed back there now." He bends over the railing again, "Well, in a minute."

Hamilton cannot sleep anymore. His head feels like a bouncing tire on a rough road. His face is two shades lighter than normal. Mr. White yells, "Gentlemen, breakfast is ready." Hamilton hears footsteps from the men headed down, but he's not moving, physically anyway.

His father walks in, "How are you feeling?"

Hamilton tries to remain still, "Okay. I will be down later."

His father smiles. "Good enough," and heads down to breakfast. The next voice Hamilton hears is, "Gentlemen, it's lunchtime."

Mr. White's words bounce slowly through his head, and finally food sounds appetizing. Hopefully it is digestible. Hamilton pushes himself up and rolls off the bed. The end of a hangover can be self-enlightening, making you feel refreshed, but the very beginning and the middle are enough to limit excessive drinking for most people.

Hamilton steps slowly towards the door, still a little queasy. A slow dose of coffee and food should perk him back to normal. The stairs slowly disappear under his feet. He approaches the dining room where the men are gathered eating their lunch.

"He's alive!" shouts Breslin and they laugh.

Grandfather tells him, "You will be a man when you can hold your whiskey, but until then the whiskey holds you".

Cleveland replies, "I wish the whiskey would let go, I don't need her company anymore! Ha-ha!" The men laugh.

"Have some coffee young man," offers Mr. White, who then picks up Hamilton's cup and pours it full.

"Thank you," says a polite, but pale, Hamilton.

Harold asks Dr. Everhart, "How is your patient?"

"Hans said he had one of his best night's sleep ever, he's doing great."

Harold replies, "Well, that is one advantage of a pharmacy head."

Doctor informs them, "He should be up and moving shortly, I gave him more pain medicine earlier. No sense in letting him suffer with pain for too long."

Grandfather laughs, "It looks like others are also suffering."

Isaac is sitting at the table, but is not his usual talkative self. Perhaps this weekend's experience has lifted him into manhood? Or it could be the hangover? It is too early to tell. The men talk for another hour. Hans is finally up and slowly walking. He makes his way into the dining room.

"Wow! It feels like a team of horses ran over me."

Mr. White asks, "Would you like breakfast or lunch?"

"Just toast."

"Here, have a seat," Harold stands up and pushes his chair out to him. Hamilton II tells them, "We had better head back soon. It is always wise to get home before dark, especially with the problems that some of these headlights have."

Breslin agrees, "I will start loading up the automobiles."

Isaac finally speaks, "I will help you." Breslin's eyes open wide with disbelief at those four words, thinking to himself, *maybe there is hope for this kid after all*.

Isaac and Breslin walk over by the door, pick up some gear, and head outside. A couple of trips and they are done. Breslin says to Hamilton II, "It looks like we are ready when you are."

Grandfather loudly asks, "Are we ready to head back to reality, commitments, and schedules?"

Harold adds, "That is life. Besides I need to make more money for my clients."

Grandfather says with much sadness, "Life's clock never stops turning... and unfortunately for me, it is almost midnight."

Cleveland comes back with an upbeat voice, "I am sure your hands of time are stuck at eleven o'clock, sir."

"I would pay a million for that!" They laugh.

"Well, let's go, shall we!" Breslin instructs. The men walk to the loaded automobiles. Isaac is automobile number one. He starts it up, and then pulls behind the others. Breslin thinks to himself, *someone had better check Isaac's temperature.* They start down the bumpy trail, bouncing around until they reach the main road.

Most of the men are quiet, some with thoughts of the tons of things they have to do when they arrive home, some with hangovers, one with pain. Hans is riding in the same automobile as Dr. Everhart and Harold. Hamilton is also quiet, but now with his hangover nearly gone, his thoughts of Emily and Dedra are alive and well; and not so well. He feels guilty for still seeing Dedra when he knows he loves Emily, but he excuses that by thinking it is not entirely his fault because she won't have physical love with him. This weekend's adventure was so affected with excitement and madness. *Hmm*, he thinks, just like his relationships with Emily and Dedra.

The more than two-hour trip seems to disappear fast like a perfect summer day. Newport is now in sight, with its inviting harbor and mooring sailboats, its wide tree-lined streets lined with priceless mansions, and its quaint Victorian-style houses.

Hamilton cannot wait to see Emily and experience her kiss, her smell, her smile, and her conversation. She is almost perfect, but the arousing thoughts of her lead him to arousing thoughts of Dedra. He can be so directly physical with her. She understands he is a man with wants and needs. But this insane spider's web is bound to trap him, he thinks, so he must tell Dedra the truth, that he does not love her. She will understand. His mind is finally made up. *The truth must be told, the truth must be told,* he says it over and over, convincing himself for the moment.

They pull into the mansion's driveway. Hamilton is looking next door trying to see if Emily is home. Dr. Everhart informs Breslin they will bring Hans home. Breslin understands, "Well, this, for the most part, was a good time. It was certainly memorable. I hope to see you men again soon," and he drives off. Cleveland, with appreciation, says to Grandfather and Hamilton II, "Thank you for sharing your hunting trip with me. Sir, I shall never forget this."

"You are welcome, son," Grandfather replies. As Cleveland walks off in the direction of the carriage house, Grandfather adds, "That young man should to go to college. He could be a great asset to the business world."

Hamilton agrees, "It is too bad he can't go."

Dr. Everhart informs them, "Harold and I will take Hans home now and explain the accident to his family."

Isaac comes over and apologizes to the men and Hans again. "Accidents happen," Harold says and adds, "The important thing is that you learn from your mistakes."

"Yes, sir." Isaac gets into the *Blue Demon* with its missing fender and drives off. Harold, Dr. Everhart, and Hans follow in Isaac's trail.

Chapter 24

The three Hamilton's enter the mansion's front door. "Good Evening," a staff member welcomes them home. "How was the hunt, sir?"

"Just fine!" Grandfather answers. The three men look at each other and smile. It took many, many years, but they have finally *bonded*. As a result, these three relatives are now friends. *Now that is precious*, Hamilton thinks, and then announces, "I am going to take a stroll along Cliffwalk." They know he probably wants to see Emily next door.

"Enjoy your walk," his father says.

It is nearly dark. A long day, and a long weekend, leave Hamilton feeling tired, but thoughts of Emily and Dedra keep his mind racing. He walks out to Cliffwalk and listens to the ocean below, the wave's crashing sounds are music to his ears. It is one of the most treasured things about being here for the summer. It is peaceful and exciting, like classical music by Mozart.

He no sooner loses those thoughts to the magic of the wave's *music* when he hears a voice, "Hamilton is that you?"

"Yes. It is me, Dedra."

"Oh! I was just thinking about you. Did you miss me?"

"I, uh, yes. How are you?"

"I am heavenly now! Did you go on your hunting trip?"

"Yes, we just returned."

"Was it successful?"

"Yes, we landed a few quail."

"Wonderful, I have missed you so much Hamilton. I think about us often! Will you see me once you go to Boston University?"

"Uh, I can probably come and visit you. Can I be truthful with you Dedra?" It is time for Hamilton to man up with the truth.

"Yes!" her voice sounds pleased that he would say that, and she is thinking commitment. "Oh! Yes! Tell me what is on your mind."

"I, uh . . . Well, I do like you a lot and have feelings for you . . ."

"Yes! Yes!"

"But . . . I do not love you totally." There is silence . . . The tears begin streaming down Dedra's face.

"Oh, Hamilton!" she breaks down. "Tell me what I have done wrong. I can change. How shall I act? Who do you want me to be? Please tell me!" She is now crying uncontrollably. Hamilton sees what he has done. Suddenly he feels like the most evil person in the world.

"You have done nothing wrong. It's me. I just cannot tell you I love you when I don't. My God, please forgive me, Dedra. I thought we were just having some foolish summer fun."

She collapses onto the ground. "Oh! Hamilton I would die for you!"

"Don't say that!" Hamilton's eyes are full of tears. "Dedra, I am sorry."

"So am I, Hamilton . . . So am I." She buries her crying head between her knees, so she won't have to look at Hamilton. Hamilton is speechless thinking, *what should I do?* The waves and Dedra's crying are the only sounds he can hear. He can feel her pain in the sound of her crying.

Hamilton kneels down next to her. "Dedra, I am truly sorry!"

"Leave me alone Hamilton! . . . Just leave me alone."

He is frozen for a minute, then finally he starts to walk away. She's still crying incessantly. Hamilton is thinking, *I cannot leave her here like this. I never meant this to happen. What should I do.* He decides he'll walk away but not too far. That way he can watch and make sure she gets home okay. He walks for a hundred feet and disappears behind a row of shrubs. He can barely see her outline, yet her crying is all he can hear.

Almost an hour passes and finally she stands up, and slowly walks along the path. Hamilton thinks she's okay now, so he makes his way back to the mansion. He feels like a monster. How could he be so cold? Why did he have to tell her the truth? Just to make himself feel better? That didn't work either—he feels worse! He reaches the mansion and sits down on the porch steps. Now what? Should he tell Emily the truth? His wave of honesty has crashed on him. Sometimes you shouldn't be truthful because it just causes pain and heartache.

He decides not to tell Emily. The summer night's warm air does little to comfort him, nor does the pleasant smell of the prized roses. He sits there for two hours collecting his thoughts, hoping Dedra is strong enough to endure this heartache caused by him. He's totally exhausted from this episode and from the trip, so he heads up to bed. But it takes him another two hours to fall asleep.

He's awakened at six-thirty a.m. by Rose's voice, "Hamilton there is a girl here to see you. I think it's the girl from next door." Hamilton is puzzled. What could she want so early in the morning? Or is it Dedra? Either way, he must go down and see.

"Thank you Aunt Rose! I'll get dressed."

"Very well!" It's a long walk down the stairs not knowing what is waiting for him. He sees it is Emily, so he gathers up a smile. But she is not smiling back.

"Hamilton, can we have a conversation?"

"Yes! Let us go outside. Sure!" He becomes anxious and nervous as Emily seems very serious.

They walk outside and sit down on the mansion's front steps.

"What's on your mind?"

"Hamilton, I hope this is not true, but do you know a girl named Dedra?"

"Yes, uh, I believe so. The one who lives a couple of blocks away just off Cliffwalk?" Hamilton's look says it all.

Emily starts crying, "Then it's true..."

"What's true?"

"You deceived and betrayed me, Hamilton," she pushes him away. "You told me all summer long you wanted to be with me, yet you were having a relationship with Dedra." Emily seems to be feeling more sorry for Dedra than herself.

"Emily, I do love you, but I also need physical love. I'm a man, I have needs..."

"You disappoint me. Only a man who can control his fires is worthy of my love. Hamilton you are not that man and you are not worthy of me or my love. The doctor is still at Dedra's house. She took all of her mother's pain medicine. Hamilton, I just hope she lives. You have really let her down. All she wanted to do was love a good man. You know her father died a few years ago. Hamilton, how could you?"

Hamilton is silent. He's finally been caught in the web he weaved, the strands of lies and deception finally connected. He now knows this is all over. A *true love* is over, and a *physical love* is over. He wrecked the lives of three people—the price of his own selfish actions.

"Emily..." he attempts one more try, "I do love you, you must know that..."

"My heart tells me to forgive you, but my mind tells me to forget you. I'm sorry Hamilton, but my mind won't disappoint me. I feel sorry for Dedra. She's very fragile. How could you? The feelings of a woman are not a toy for you to play with; they come with a great deal of responsibility. This you will learn someday. Dedra didn't want to tell me who it was that broke her heart. I wouldn't leave until she told me. It shocked me to find out it was you, Hamilton." With that she walks away, taking

Hamilton's heart with her. He is devastated. He just shakes his head back and forth, but this bad dream is real.

Hamilton remembers from the jazz ball that Emily and Dedra are friends. He can't help but think that telling Dedra was a stupid mistake, or was the whole idea of this *love triangle* the mistake? At this point it doesn't matter, the damage is done.

Rose wheels over to the front door and can see through the side glass panels that Hamilton is sitting on the front steps. She manages to open the door wide enough to ask Hamilton, "Is anything wrong?"

"Yes. Right now everything is wrong. I'll tell you later, Aunt Rose."

"Let me know when you're ready. Talking can help."

But Hamilton knows Rose will think less of him for this selfish series of events. She always teaches that one must be respectful of others, and right now Hamilton doesn't even respect himself. Hamilton sits for another hour, then goes inside, and up to his bedroom.

Chapter 25

All Hamilton can do is lie in bed and think about the damage he's caused. He's lost the one person he cares the most about. It's now past eight a.m. He hears Rose yell, "Hamilton come quickly." He jumps out of bed and runs out into the hall.

"Father's not up yet and there's no answer from his room. I can't open the door. He's usually up before six a.m." Hamilton's heart sinks. He opens the door slowly, while calling out his name.

"Grandfather, Grandfather," he walks over to the bed. Still he doesn't move. He reaches down to shake him a little, but as he does, he feels his cold skin. Hamilton kneels on the floor and starts to cry and gives him a final hug.

"Oh, Rose, he's gone."

She is near the bed and reaches out to Hamilton and her father, "Run to mother, run to mother. We love you," she says hoping they are reuniting in the afterlife. The tears fall down their faces.

Grandfather was a caring and compassionate person towards the end of his life, but when he was younger he was tough and all-business. Age has a way of taming a man, either by experience, knowledge, or just tiredness. Maybe all three. They send Cleveland Sr. to find Hamilton II, who is already at his office. Young Cleveland's eyes are also full of tears; he had more than a *work* relationship with Grandfather. Hamilton I had always given Cleveland's father extra money around the holidays, and Cleveland himself had just spent the past weekend with him hunting.

"I'm sorry, Hamilton."

"Thank you . . . My grandfather had a good, long life." Soon Hamilton II comes in, as does Dr. Everhart who checks him over and says, "A lucky man dies in his sleep. No pain, no suffering. He's at peace now and can probably already hear the harps of heaven."

Hamilton II says, "I'll call Epelaus Funeral Service."

The news travels fast and by noon the house is full of people paying their respects and offering help if it is needed. The mansion has a steady flow of people for two days. On the third day, they hold funeral services and the burial. One week later, the family receives a letter from the family lawyer, H. L. Steinbach:

> "Dear Mr. Hamilton Morgan Slate II,
>
> I am sorry for your loss. We request your presence this coming Tuesday for the reading of your father's will. Rose, Hamilton III, Cleveland Roosevelt Sr., Cleveland Roosevelt Jr., and Mr. Bremhan are also requested to be present."

Tuesday comes. They climb into the Duisenberg with Cleveland Sr. driving. They are heart-broken to know Hamilton I is gone, but they are also anxious to know why all of them need to be present concerning the will. There is a parking spot open directly in front of the lawyer's office. In they go.

"We are here to see Mr. Steinbach."

"Please have a seat I'll let him know you're here." They walk over to the bench and before they can sit down, Mr. Steinbach comes out of his office, "I'm sorry for your loss. Hamilton was a successful and well-respected man."

"Thank you," says Hamilton II. Hamilton is pushing Rose's wheelchair so she can navigate around piles of law books stacked upon the floor. The one and only time she has let him.

"Excuse the mess. I just moved into this office from next door. Please have a seat," he points to the chairs in front of his desk. "Hamilton accomplished a lot in his lifetime; he made a fortune and provided well for his family. Quite recently, he had me make a couple of changes to his will. I will read them to you as he wanted them read:

> "The first change (their wide eyes can hardly wait) is that Cleveland Roosevelt Sr. will be provided a retirement allowance. He will be given $500 a month so he can fish from sunrise to sunset. He is more than a long-term employee. I found him to be a good friend. Cleveland, go catch a big one."

You can see how pleased Cleveland is, as he has tears of joy. He sits speechless.

"Next Olive Rose, my lovely breathe of fresh air, I leave twenty-five percent of the company to you and I expect your brother and nephew to help you throughout your entire life. I know they will."

"Hamilton, my son, you shall run the company and you now own fifty-one percent of it. I wish you continued success. Preserve our fortune."

They are all thinking, *Where's the other twenty-four percent?*

"Hamilton, my grandson, I want you also involved in the company. But first you must finish college and when you have graduated you shall have the remaining twenty-four percent ownership. Study hard."

Hamilton doesn't have any words to say.

"Now, Cleveland Roosevelt Jr., although I don't know you very well, I am impressed by your sound character and your thirst for knowledge. It would be a waste of your life and God-given talents to just drive automobiles for the rest of your life. You now have four years of college all paid for. I only ask that you work hard. I know you will."

Cleveland is also lost for words, but finds a few tears.

Mr. Steinbach keeps reading:

"The household staff shall divide $50,000 evenly amongst themselves. I owe them a great deal of gratitude.'

"Lastly, my assistant Mr. Bremhan, you now have the keys to an ocean-view home, along with $25,000. It's time for you to relax. You are a good man who made my life easier."

The Attorney excuses himself, "I'll give you some time to digest all of this." They just look at each other. They are both stunned and pleased. Fifteen minutes later the lawyer comes back into the room and asks them if they have any questions concerning the will. They all answer no. Mr. Steinbach says that if they do have questions later, they can contact him by mail.

They slowly file out of the office and climb into the automobile. Cleveland Sr. starts it up and they head for home. They are all very sad, but are pleased and surprised with the words of the will. No one has been hurt by this reading and it seems like they have all benefited from it.

Cleveland Sr. proudly announces, "I think I will take tomorrow off from work. Oh, and the tomorrow after that . . . to fish. I can't rightly say if I will ever come back, so do not think I'ze fallin' in and drowned." He has a couple of tears rolling down his face and says, "I sure do miss Mr. Slate." On the drive home, the others let out a few tears as well.

As they walk through the front door, the mansion seems empty without Hamilton I. At this moment, Hamilton is also painfully missing Emily—her priceless and pure smile, her laugh, her beauty, her words, all of her. Now two of the most important people are forever gone from his life.

Yet, several boys grew into men this summer—one was bruised, but not broken; another lost his selfish ways and found a few new friends; one found a taste of the good life which forever changed his life. But Hamilton, it seems, learned life's most painful lesson: you can have it all . . . you just can't have it all. You can never truly control your own universe, because the planets are constantly rearranging.

Some things are always just beyond your control, and some things are always just beyond your understanding. That is what makes life . . . life.

Get Published, Inc!
Thorofare, NJ 08086
29 September 2009
BA2009272